The Lawyer's Luck

A Home to Milford College prequel novella

By Piper Huguley

Liliaceae Press

Cover by JShan
Editors: Sally Bradley and Bev Harrison

ACKNOWLEDGEMENTS

First of all, I would like to thank God for helping to know and understand my purpose in life. I've bumbled though life for so long, looking for the right thing to do. I have to let folks know how grateful I am to have found a purpose for my work. Thank you.

My parents helped me to understand that purpose. Mom and Dad, thank you so much for everything and every little bit of support that you have given to me. I love you—always.

To Marcus Riggins, I know you don't understand a lot of what I do, but thank you for being there for me while I was trying to find my purpose.

Xavier Riggins, you are the shining star of my world. One day, I hope you will come to understand what I do and why I do it. And be proud of me.

To the family who supported me: Anna K. Comer, Johnnie and Jean Comer, the various Holt cousins, Heather and Elmer Harris, Kenny and Letitia Riggins and Veronica Riggins. Thank you.

Thank you so much to the following writer friends who made me believe it was all possible: Julie Hilton Steele, Vanessa Riley, Parker J. Cole, Kennedy Ryan, Barbara Andrews, Mary

Anne Lewis, Diana Rubino, Preslaysa Williams, Jamie Wesley, Sonali Dev, the History Lovers, the Seekers at Seekerville, the Lucky 13s, the Dreamweavers and the readers and writers at Romance Slam Jam.

This book and everything I write will be forever dedicated to the wondrous Lilia C. Huguley. I would be nothing without you. Thank you for pouring your heart and soul into me and for reminding me we must celebrate and uplift those who came before us and dared to survive. I live in the hope that I will continue to reflect the very best of you.

Chapter One

June, 1844—somewhere near Elyria, Ohio

A lawyer, riding circuit, must have a horse. So where was his? Did it wander off?

Lawrence Stewart replanted his feet, making impatient thudding noises on the wooden porch of the tavern while he searched in vain for the gray dapple mare he'd rented. He wasn't a lawyer yet, still studying to be one, but how could he, such a smart man, allow the horse to wander off? Was this a sign from God that all his studying was in vain?

He stepped off the porch, pistol in hand. Just in case. Horse thieves hung around taverns, but he was ready. He needed to be prepared to face a horrific thief. Bulky, he could fight any man in hand-to-hand combat if needed, but he wasn't taking any chances. He had to get back to his circuit.

His hands felt slick to him as he held the pistol at the ready.

Ah. The horse's tracks went deep into the woods behind the tavern, northward. Praise God.

Fool thief or horse wouldn't get that far going through the woods.

Still, if he followed these tracks, he would be late with his next circuit court, in the opposite direction. How those in some small Ohio settlement would love to write a letter to Charles, telling him that his experiment to have a graduate fresh out of Oberlin—especially a Negro with Miami nation blood running through his veins—hadn't worked No matter that he was the first in his class, they would love to say he'd failed. Two reasons warred in his blood to prove to settlers he should not be trusted.

He waded through the thick foliage. Plenty of daylight still left, even though the more he went into the forest, he could see less of it. If he rode like Lucifer, he could still make his circuit.

Still, whoever took his horse was desperate—which he didn't like. Desperation meant more danger for him.

More danger *to* him.

He had to have that horse back.

Fortunately, the forest was so thick in this part of the country that the sun was blocked out, leaving only traces of the pungent smell of fish nearby to guide him. Lake Huron loomed ahead. Where was the horse? The horse, if it wandered off, would stay on the road. His heart thudded hard in him.

Who would dare take his horse—what was its name? Beauty? Beauregard? He *had* to get it back. He wouldn't have enough money to pay for another until after he passed his exams, the ones he had studied years for. If he passed them, he might have a horse of his own.

"Beautiful? Biscayne?" he called out. Would the horse respond?

Thuds on the soft forest grass sounded and then stopped. Lawrence smiled. There was always something satisfying about justice. His aim was to be in a courtroom handing out justice, in a new Prince Albert suit. Not sweating in the sun in a stifling white shirt and buckskins. But still. Satisfying.

He cocked his pistol and held it out in front of him and spoke in a loud, steady voice he did not feel at the moment. "I have no quarrel with you, whoever you are. All I want is the horse. I have important business, and I must be on my way."

The horse nickered.

"I don't have money, either, so don't think you're going to get that. I just want the horse."

He inched closer, and there was the dapple gray tied to a tree in the clearing. It was as he thought. Stolen. Still, the horse stood placid and sure. She wasn't going anywhere. He lowered the gun to puzzle at the situation. How peculiar. Why steal his horse and tie it up out here? That made no sense.

No matter. Time to get Bulgaria and be on his way. He hurried to the horse.

Something attacked his jaw, blindsiding him.

Thank goodness he had a small growth of beard so the blow didn't hit him that hard, but it still knocked him back and the cocked gun in his hand went off; the shot echoed in the forest and the gun thunked on the soft forest floor.

A clear female voice rang out into the dim light. "Yeow! Master God!"

Lawrence sprang to his feet, feeling his body. The bullet hadn't grazed *him* but the person who had shouted. A woman. A female here in the woods.

The knight in him couldn't resist. He went to the source of the voice, making out the crouched figure of a small woman dressed in dark, dowdy men's clothing, clutching her arm. Blood ran through her fingers.

Icy cold fear gripped his stomach, and he wanted to cry out to God for forgiveness. He had shot a woman. A man couldn't get much lower than shooting a defenseless woman. He fell to his knees next to her. His voice, rasped with guilt, answered her. "Ma'am, you've been shot. Let me assist you."

"Keep on away from me, cur! Shooting on me! Yous hell bound today."

Lawrence didn't know what shocked him more. The thought of going to Lucifer's home and his dread fear of it? Was it that this petite woman called him names and cursed him? Or was it the tinkling musicality of her voice? Was it that she was obviously a runaway slave, or the raw beauty reflected in her large eyes framed by delicate, dark brown features? Or was it that she hardly had any hair on her head? His mind was a mixture of emotions, and he wished he was in some classroom in Oberlin, poring over a book with cases in it. He would feel immensely more comfortable.

"Miss, there's no need for that kind of language. Clearly, you're in need of assistance."

"Don't need 'sistance."

More blood spurted from her.

"Seems to me that you do." Couldn't take off his buckskins. He had nothing on him but his free-trade cotton shirt. He had another back at the tavern, so he would use this one to rip it into strips and bind her arm until they got help. He grasped at the bottom of the shirt and yanked it off.

"Hold there!" The strange woman spoke out loud, her pretty voice echoing through the stand of trees. "Didn't ask you to undress."

Lawrence gritted his teeth. "I'm ripping up my shirt to make a tourniquet for your arm. Do you mind?"

"I do it. Don't want no strange man touching on me."

Lord Almighty, this young woman frustrated him no end, but he knew what was right to do. He kept going, the need to be quick coursing through his veins. Sometimes he called it the Miami in him, having foresight and vision to see what was ahead. He spoke on. "You need help. You cannot do your own tourniquet."

The woman sagged against the tree, seeming to be at peace with his words. He certainly hoped so. What else was she going to do?

He took the strips and began to bind the woman's arm as hard as he could. She didn't move her hand from the wound until the last possible moment, then slipped her hand away and let him work.

Her energy slipped as the blood spurted out in an alarming, rhythmic fashion. As a heartbeat would. She needed more help, that was certain. He had to get her back to the tavern.

Lawrence spoke to distract her. "Thank goodness I came out here. I was in search of my horse—someone stole it, then tied it up here. Very strange happening. When I get a hold of that thief, I have something for him. Horse thieving is a hanging offense."

The woman's arm warmed under her dirty brown coat. Her head lolled away from him. Not so feisty now, she seemed to scold him. "What you going to wear now?"

"I have another shirt at the tavern. We have to get you back there so you can get real help. This binding is only temporary."

"Why your kind so foolish?"

"My kind?" Lawrence stopped his ministrations and stared at her. "We both have skins of brown as I see it."

The woman held up her other hand, which was beginning to cake with dried blood. "I mean *men*. You took off your shirt to help me. Why should you do it?"

"I'm a Christian. I would help you. That's what God says is my duty."

The woman turned from him and spat in the dirt. Heavens, she spit as well as any man. "God don't have nothing to do with anything," she said.

"How can you say that? He has everything to do with everything. God is our creator."

Her dark eyes fixed on him, glaring, seeming to want to tear him to strips. "I says that because I almost got to Canada. Almost to freedom and I'm up here in the woods, fooling with you."

Lawrence nodded. "You're close."

"Now you're going to take me back." She sagged and her bright eyes dimmed a bit. "Beaten down by a fancy man."

"What does that mean? I'm no fancy man."

The woman perked a bit. "You talk like one."

"I'm a lawyer. Words are my profession."

She shook her head. "I don't know what that means. You is either fancy, dressing up what you say with prettiness, or you plain. Like me. Say what you mean straight."

"My words are not pretty." Lawrence bristled as he contemplated the next step. How would he get her out of here?

"Then say what you mean, man." The woman spat her words at him, just as she had spat in the dirt a few minutes ago.

He paid her no attention. What a terrible mess this beautiful woman was with her dirty, smelly clothes and curt ways. She would be a burden to anyone willing to take her on. Clearly, a task for someone else, not him. Belastrode would help him get her to help at the tavern, he would get his things, and go on to the circuit.

Striding over to the patiently waiting horse, he untied the reins from the tree. "Come on, Barony." The horse followed him, with chopping, halting steps. He yanked at the reins a little and felt a resistance from the horse. Who was in charge here anyway? He led the horse as close as he could to where the woman still sat, not running away and no longer bleeding, but a corona of anger fairly glowed from her rich brown skin.

"Can you get up on the horse? If you can, then we'll get you to the tavern much faster. What do you think?"

The woman scrabbled around in the dirt and branches and pulled herself up on her knees. Her dark eyes didn't seem steady to him though, and there was a thin sheen of sweat on her fine sienna-brown features.

She tried to pull herself up but wasn't able to. He caught her, and taking care of her arm, picked her up and plunked her on the horse. "Hold on with your good hand and sit up."

"I'm doing what I can."

She was so light in his arms. No wonder she had such a poor attitude. When had she had a good meal? It made him snappish to miss one meal, and with as many meals as this woman probably missed, she was not very happy at all.

The woman made some low nicking sounds in her throat.

The horse went on, taking careful steps as if she knew the woman were hurt.

Bremerton had started right up at her command. That horse never wanted to do as he said. "How did you do that?"

"Horse got to know you respect it, Mr. Fancy Man. This here horse don't feel respect from you. That's how come she go with me. She like how she feel being with me. Hadn't been for you, we could been crossed into Canada, both of us free."

The impertinent woman slid herself down and lay flat out on the horse without falling. He took a step back, watching the horse taking dainty steps to pick her way through the woods so as to not throw off the load of the lightweight, snappish woman.

"The horse isn't mine."

"Still. No respect. You don't even know her name."

He opened his mouth to deny it, but she spoke the truth. "It's a horse. What difference what she's called?"

The woman lifted her head a bit. The dark glares from her eyes came right back at him. The glares sliced his heart, as if she could cut a heart shape and lift that piece of his anatomy out. "Got a brown skin, but you sounds like Old Frank Milford. He could never recall our names either."

As strongly as if a gavel had hit him upside the head, he realized with some shame that he didn't know the woman's name. He hadn't even paid her the decent human respect of asking her name.

"I'm Lawrence."

The woman scoffed.

"What's wrong with that?"

"Fancy name."

"It's what I was christened. Lawrence Stewart." Not Dark Wolf.

She turned away from him, cradling her arm to her body. As she did, the back of the tavern emerged. Thank God. He could turn over the care of this belligerent woman to someone else.

"I'm calling you Lawyer."

He cleared his throat. "That's what I do, madam. It's not who I am. The tavern is over here. We'll get you help and you'll feel better soon. What's your name?"

She edged herself off of the horse's back and sagged, the blood loss giving her features a tinge of gray that didn't look healthy. "They going to sell me back south."

He reached out a hand to her and stopped himself, knowing it would be inappropriate to touch this woman. "I'll stay and help you. It will be all right, but you need the right bandages, food, clean clothing, and"—he wrinkled his nose—"a bath for you."

"My name Realie."

Really? Realie? What kind of a name was that?

He tied the horse to the post and patted Bessie's nose. She looked completely indifferent at his touch. Realie had a point. The horse knew he didn't care for it. Resolving to do better, he picked up the light woman and, holding her close, carried her into the tavern, hoping they would help her and him.

Now he had less time than ever to get to his next court circuit. No doubt he would lose his job.

CHAPTER TWO

Only time she ever been hotter than now was in the sweatbox. She only been punished like only one time.

Time before she ran off.

That had settled the question for her. Nobody, *nobody,* was going to treat Aurelia any kind of way.

Not even her mistress.

Milly thought she would show Realie a thing or two. Turned out the other way.

Lying on the hot bed in the tavern, twisting this way and that, the tickling started deep in her throat and bloomed into a cough. She tried to roll over, but the patched-up quilt stuck to her body, drenched with her own sweat and spicy stink. "Ain't there any water around here? What kind a place is this?"

The fancy man from the woods came with water in a carved wooden dipper. "Here, drink some of this."

The warm water looked brown and smelled like rotted fish. Realie held up her hand. "I sooner drink piss."

The fancy man turned from her, his handsome features all knitted up like some of Milly's hand mitts. "Your wound is getting better."

She touched her arm and found it heavily bandaged. "Good. Got to get to Canada 'fore nightfall."

"There's no Canada for you…Realie." He hesitated before he said her name, as if it were some mixed-up French Milly talk.

She tried to pull herself up again, but she wasn't wearing her traveling clothes. Somehow she was in a shift. How did that get on her? She wanted to bolt, to get away from him, but not knowing how she'd gotten into the shift was sure mortification.

"You report me?" she asked.

"No." The fancy man gave her some buttered bread. "Eat some of this for strength. If you don't want the water, there's broth here to help you swallow the bread."

With her good hand, she took the bread. "Plenty of money for catching one like me. You rich?"

A slow smile featuring shiny white teeth spread across his face. He was a rich tan color, like Milly's favorite riding horse, Honey Child. And his pretty hair. His curls looked like silk to the touch, not nappy ones. "No, Realie. I'm not rich."

Humph. Fancy man a liar too. Which was why she had to get away from him. Never seen no slave man wearing such nice brown pants, fitting up on his body tight and snug. That shirt looked like he got it from a store. Made from fine material. Not slave cloth woven quick from the cotton. Store bought. His black eyes were shiny and clear. No one ever clouted him before.

He was rich; he just didn't know it.

"You a slave?"

"No. I'm a lawyer. Well, I hope to be one soon."

"What you mean?"

"Well, Realie, when you stole my horse, I was studying for exams. I get a lot of studying done while I ride circuit for Judge Henry since his health won't allow it."

"How else am I supposed to get into Canada? Walk? Should have treated that horsey better. She know what to do."

"Forgive me if I'm not good with animals."

"Nothing to forgive. You just don't know much, Lawyer."

"Did you take care of the horses where you came from?"

Time to shut her mouth. She put some bread in her mouth, saying nothing. Gotta be careful around one such as him. You could see he was smart. How else he get all those clothes and teeth?

She lowered her eyes and refused to lift them as she ate heartily of the bread and butter. The greasy broth was in a carved wood bowl. It was awkward to use the spoon with her left hand, but she fed herself. The broth was cold, but it did help to soften the lump of bread in her throat and was better than the water.

He broke the quiet with his deep voice. "So you have nothing to say."

"I'm eating. Got to get my strength up for Canada."

"Like I said, no Canada for you."

"You stopping me?"

"Didn't say that. You have to use your energy to get well."

"You expect me to stay in this bed while the catchers come? You crazy! I've got to get up out of here."

She set the tray with the empty bowl aside and tried to move her sticky legs to the edge of the bed. She pushed herself to stand, but everything look sideways. Not right at all. She sat back down.

Lawyer said nothing. He got the tray and left the room.

How come she feeling this way? Tears sprang to her eyes, but she whisked them away.

He came back to see her perched on the side of the crude bed. "You rest. I have to convene court."

"You leaving me here? For the catchers?"

He eased her down on the bed. Realie lifted the corner of the quilt. Did feel better to lie here.

"No catchers will come."

"How come you so sure?"

"I told them you were my wife, and I had to shoot you to keep you in one place."

"You say what?" Realie shot up. The broth and bread threatened to come right back up, and she lay down, defeated.

Lawyer showed her those pretty teeth of his. Lord a mercy. "It's not legal, but men around these parts aren't averse to using a gun to keep their wives under control. I've had to settle many a dispute."

"You nigh killed me."

The shiny black eyes in his handsome face got to be real small. "You stole my horse. If I reported you to the proper authorities, you would be tried in circuit court and hanged."

She swallowed the last thick lump of bread in her throat. The place a rope would go if she were hanged, and she sweated some more.

"Good thing for you that I'm the circuit court around here."

"I don't even know what you are talking about, man."

Lawyer picked up a long black coat and shrugged himself into it. Looked store bought too. Someone sewing lots for him. Or he got money to buy nice clothes. Had to cut the shoulders and arms extra wide to fit himself into it. She hated sewing, but she knew that much. "Part of my lawyer training is to ride the circuit. I go around this area of north Ohio for Judge Henry. People can't get to a courthouse all the time, so they wait for me to come. I get around about every other month."

"Since when they let a brown man do that?"

Lawyer shook his head, and she sat up straighter to see his silky curls dancing. "I haven't said it's been easy. I've only gotten started. Some of the settlers are still a little hostile, but it's what I have to do."

"You must be mighty important."

The black eyes focused over her shoulder. What was he thinking of? "It's all part of what has to be done to protect my people."

"You got a woman sewing your clothes for you?"

"A woman? I'm a Christian." Lawyer seemed confused as he adjusted himself.

She shook her head. "No, I mean a wife. You married?"

He showed off those teeth again. Man seemed kind of full of himself, come to notice. But he had a right to be. She ain't never seen the like of him before.

"No, you're it, far as I can tell."

"No need of you telling lies like that."

He touched the bandage on her arm and she wanted to wiggle away from him, but she didn't because the warmth spread through her from his fingers. "I'm going to be gone for two days. Then I'll be back. Mrs. Taylor—she'll be up to change your dressing. She's the owner's wife. She knows me."

"Then she know you don't have a wife."

He patted her hand after examining her bandage. "Men who ride the circuit have wives they leave behind. That's what I told her. I had left you behind and you came after me, trying to haul me home. Had to shoot you to calm you down."

"I sees."

"That's why you can be in here with me. They know I'm a Christian man."

"You so Christian, who put this here shift on me?"

"That belongs to Mrs. Taylor."

"Didn't ask who it belong to. I asked who put me in it?"

Lawyer walked to the door and spoke in a gentle voice. "You were knocked out. I put it on with my eyes closed. I wouldn't take advantage of you in any way."

The broth and bread went to swimming in her stomach again. Best stay still.

"I'll see you in two days." Lawyer opened the door and walked out, leaving her alone.

She gulped and clutched the shift closer at the thought. Did it make any difference anyhow? She'd give away anything she had—anything to stay free of Milly and her sweatbox ways.

Still, the small room was like a sweatbox. She slept on, tossing and turning. Dreams seemed so real, it was like she'd stepped back to Georgia. Dreamt of her mama with belly all big with another baby. Number nineteen. God with her, she would never see this baby her mam was about to bear.

Her body wanted to sink through the itchy ticking and rope ties. She kicked her legs out in rebellion at her fate. Mam had told her what to do. She wanted her to get away, to not serve Milly anymore. And she almost did it. She'd almost made it. Mam would be proud of how far she'd come. She wouldn't have to go back. Would she?

The nightmare made her sit straight up in bed. She touched her face. Was it sweat or tears?

She was powerful thirsty. Nasty water seemed good now.

Problem was, it was on a table across the room. Fancy lawyer man didn't bring it to her. She'd have to get it herself.

Swinging her legs to the side, she took in a deep fetid breath. *Gotta do this.* She pushed off on the wooden posts that framed the bed ties and stood. Her legs were like Honey Child's when she was a colt. *Gotta do this.*

Legs were not going to help her. Great. She fell to her knees, which made a loud sound on the hardwood floor. Why was there so much wood around here? They needed some carpets. Like what Milly had.

Her knees made little stings to her stomach as she crawled on the wood, but she got to the table and lifted up the wood dipper out of the pan on top of the table. She held her nose and took a deep gulp. The dipper was only half full, but the water slid down into her. Whew. Better than nothing. At least her lips weren't hard and crusty anymore.

She sat there on the floor for a long time. Didn't have strength to go back. Seemed mighty fine to just stretch out on the floor and sleep. She had slept on worse, trying to get up to Ohio. Her knees were bleeding a little, but she would take care of that. Later. She stretched her body out and curled up into a ball, relieved to be out of that sweatbox bed.

She was woken up when a young woman came into the room and put another tray on the table. "Oh, I just knew he shouldn't have left you here alone. I was busy down in the kitchen. Couldn't come sooner."

"I'm fine, ma'am." How instantly she could go back to the old way. She knew better. This one with china-blue doll eyes and brown curls covered with a cap could be tricky.

"You need to get back into bed."

The woman hesitated though. Humph. Realie knew why. She wasn't looking to help her back. Didn't want to touch her. That's how they kept you in your place. Let you know you wasn't human. Not fit to be touched.

She crawled on her hands and bloody knees and pushed herself back to the bed while Mrs. Taylor watched. When she was on the bed ties, she stretched out, and Mrs. Taylor was willing to lift the quilt over her. "There. I brought you some beef soup."

"I wants some food."

"Got to get better a little at a time."

"Thought my husband paid for food." Realie was surprised to see the woman's china-blue eyes narrow a bit.

Then Mrs. Taylor perked up a little. "No, just soup for now." She set the tray on Realie's legs.

"I can handle this myself."

The woman looked relieved. "I'll leave you to it then."

She bustled out in her light blue dress, and Realie stared after her. Humph. Lawyer said these folk knew him and trusted him, but she had seen too much in her escape and before that to trust anyone. Best to eat this soup and find a way to get on out of here before Lawyer came back. She didn't trust him either.

Chapter Three

Haunted by thoughts of Realie, Lawrence tried his best to return during the day, but it wasn't possible. He didn't reach the tavern until the next night. Poor horse, poor... Beautiful? Appalled that he still couldn't remember the horse's name, he chalked it up to being so busy studying for the oral part of his exams.

Once he finished his exams, he would be able to come back to tell the people on the circuit so. The people thought him some type of pretender, a half-black, one-quarter Miami, one-quarter white man who didn't know anything. One advantage of walking in multiple worlds was the ability to speak more than one language. He could mete out justice in French if he had to. So he could settle disputes with some ease, and both sides would come away happy.

Besides, he couldn't stop thinking about Realie all day long. It gnawed him in the gut that he'd shot her, but she could have gotten much worse if he'd proclaimed her a horse thief. Since she was, technically, a thief—even if she didn't get far. She was really just a desperate kid.

Enslaved persons like Realie reminded him of why he was a lawyer. Slavery was an abject evil and had to be done away with, bit by bit. So if he were depriving her owner of free labor from her, he wasn't a thief. They were. Just as his grandmother's people were driven away from their land, little by little. He was put on earth to do something about that.

So, with swift trembling fingers, he tied up the horse. Bountiful? He went into the tavern where Mrs. Taylor wiped furiously at crumbs on the table.

"Ah. Mr. Stewart."

"I'm back. Thank you for watching my wife." He pulled out some additional coins and handed them to the tavern keeper.

He couldn't miss that show she made of putting the coins into her ample bosom. He looked away. Mrs. Taylor made no secret that she was willing to participate in other services. He swallowed the sick he felt rising in his throat. Guess she thought he was good-looking and wouldn't mind having relations with him. To take advantage of a woman's person like that? To abuse the special thing that God had made a woman for? He wouldn't do it.

"It's not a problem, sir."

"I'll just be on my way to seeing to her."

"Your wife." Her tone meant she didn't believe a word of what he'd told her about Realie. "She's a wild one, that."

He coughed. "Surely."

"Too wild for such a domesticated man as yourself."

"Well, we all get what we deserve in marriage, Mrs. Taylor." He stepped from the room. "Excuse me."

He refrained from running up the stairs this late at night, but his heavy-soled boots made noise that resonated throughout the hallways. He opened his door to see Realie resting in bed, her head tilted to one side, asleep.

Her dark brown skin carried a clear undertone of red—a good color that showed her to be healthy. Clearly she'd needed rest after such a remarkable journey. How had she made it all the way to Ohio from Georgia?

A bit of cloth was caught in her roughly chopped hair, and he picked it off. With no warning, she grabbed his wrist. The connection between them was immediate and nearly burned him. He might have pulled away, but something stopped him, and instead he traced his hand down the side of her face.

She jerked back as if she were burned.

Lawrence let her go. "I apologize."

He walked to the other side of the room to get her some water. When he remembered how she had reacted to it before, he set the carved pitcher down.

He watched her struggle to sit up, not wanting to touch her again because he was afraid of the warmth in his hands whenever he did. She had said nothing about his apology, and so he guessed they would act as if what had gone on between them hadn't happened.

Except she was unbuttoning her nightgown.

"Realie, what are you doing? Cease that at once."

She stopped at the fourth button. "You like the rest. You ain't being nice just because?"

She continued to unbutton, and he rushed forward to stop her, except he remembered what happened when he'd touched her before and fell back. "I'm just a man trying to do God's work. Please. Stay dressed."

She stopped and shrugged her shoulders. "Fine. However you want it."

His heart beat in horror at the thought that this young woman couldn't rest in her sleep. "Is that what enslavement was like? Who would come for you? Old Frank?"

"No. Milly would bash his head in for sure. He half scared of her. Overseer. Some other slave man. They have say over us too."

What an awful life. *Dear God, I vow to help more than ever.*

She eyed him. "Ain't nothing you ever faced."

"No, certainly not. But that doesn't mean I haven't had terrors in my life. You... you rest. I won't disturb you anymore. I'll light a candle and study some, but you go back to sleep."

He sat down at the table where the water pitcher rested and organized some cases. Might as well get in some studying before dawn came.

Dawn came too soon. Seemed like minutes later and the sun was rising. Even more strange was that Realie stood, looking out of the window. He hadn't even heard her stir.

Her bare legs exposed beneath the shift were so thin. It wasn't fair that this beautiful young woman had to struggle in such a hard life. "You aren't strong enough to be standing."

"I'm standing here, Lawyer."

"I see. Well, maybe Mrs. Taylor could bring you heartier fare today."

A wrinkle appeared on the crest of her forehead. "You sleep any?"

"Some days I don't get sleep. It happens."

"Why wouldn't a fancy man like you sleep?"

"I'm working and studying for my exams. I have things to do."

"A body got to rest sometimes. You got to take care of yourself."

Imagine her worrying about him! Strange to think that anyone could worry about him. He stood up and ran a hand over his hair. "I'll be right back."

He moved down the hall past the stink of unwashed men and down the carved wooden stairs. Mrs. Taylor eyed him. Right in front of her he did up the front laces of his shirt.

"Long night for you, Mr. Stewart."

"I've got to study, ma'am. My exams are coming up."

"Well, must be hard on a man with a brand-new wife such as you have. She's very dark but very pretty, to be sure."

For some strange reason, this woman's words woke rage within him. "We are as God fashioned us. My wife came from a very long way. She's brave and she's bold. Does that not make her beautiful as well?"

He realized too late that the words were spoken with a raw passion that did not suit him.

"Hmm. Well, I knew you were riding more circuit today, so I packed up your breakfast. You'll probably be wanting something for her too?"

"I'll pay you, of course. She may just need some bread and cheese. A piece of fruit."

"I have sliced chicken this morning."

"Just add it to my bill and I'll pay for it when I ride out."

"Sure, and it's no problem."

Mrs. Taylor fixed another tray and handed it to him. She pressed her moist hands on top of his. "She's lucky. What I wouldn't give for an attentive man for my husband," she whispered in a hot, heavy breath in his ear.

He took the tray from her and fixed her with a firm glance. "I'll bring the money down when I leave. Thank you."

In the room, Realie sat at the table, as if she were ready to eat. He smiled at her. "You look fine, my dear. I brought bread, cheese, slices of chicken, and some apple cider to wash it down." He put the tray on the table. "Let's pray. Dear Lord. Help us to do what you have set before us as a task. Let us behave in your will and do as you will, every day, every hour. In your name, for you and the Son you sacrificed for us. Amen"

When he lifted his head, she'd nearly consumed her share of the food as if someone would take it away.

"Glad to see your appetite is back."

"Back where I'm from, you don't eat, the food be gone. No time for long praying."

"I got the impression you were a lady's maid."

"No matter. Mam's going to have her nineteenth baby any day now. Too many people. Too little food."

"I thought the house slaves..." He thought about what he was going to say. The last person he wanted to offend was Realie. "I thought the house servants ate in the house. With the master."

"Them the kind of fairy stories they tell up here in the north?" She chewed on a sliver of chicken. "Where you hear that?"

His head was too full of torts and tax law. "The newspapers, most likely."

"Lies. All of it. Some days I'm so glad I can't read. Seems as if your head just get full up with nonsense and can't see your way clear to nothing."

He chewed his bread and cheese. A wise point. "So you ate with your family?"

Her beautiful brown eyes softened. "Yeah. They could all eat a lot. Wouldn't believe the spread you brought."

He tried to straighten from his slouch. All of a sudden, he wanted to know more about her. Her eyes had reflected slavery, that keen mystery that reflected his paternal side. She intrigued him in every sense of the word. "Not the kind of thing you eat at home?"

"Not chicken. No how. We catch and eat a lot of fish since Milford House is by the water." She looked off in the distance and picked up her cup. "I didn't want to leave my mother in her time of need, me being the oldest girl and all. But I know what she want me to do. I had to go. For me and my children to be free."

He gulped hard on the cider, not sure how to say what he wanted to say. No use in offending Realie, but he had to know. "How did your mother get so many children?"

Her brown eyes snapped out of their reverie and stared at him. "What you mean, Lawyer?"

"You've told me she's going to have number nineteen. That's a considerable amount of children."

"Sure is. Master, I mean Old Frank Milford call her his moneymaker. She getting old though. Near worn out." Realie shook her head and ripped the bread, making a little sandwich with the cheese and chicken. She picked up a poker and stuck the creation at the end, warming it in the fire. Smart.

"Are they Mr. Milford's children?"

Realie jumped as if the poker burned her, which wasn't the case since she held the cool end. "What you saying about my mother?"

"I thought he called her his moneymaker."

Realie calmed down. "Naw. We all belongs to my pappy. Folks say I look like him the most out of the whole bunch. We the closest in color."

He watched her features, trying to imagine a man's face in them. No. He didn't have the capability. Her delicate features wouldn't allow it. She was just too pretty. "I see. So many children, it must be hard to keep them all together."

"Oh no. We all live there. Together. Guess that was a good thing, I suppose?" She toasted her creation thoughtfully. "Milly, she come down from the north a few years back. Mr. Milford marry her cause she an older lady with a big old fortune. A widow woman. Didn't think she would have no kids, but two came right off, old as she was. She needed a lady's maid and a nanny for her two boys, so there's me. Everyone knows I'm used to caring for kids, ever since I was a little one myself. I cook meals, change diapers. Whatever need to be done. So I get pulled from my family to come live with her and sleep on the floor next to her."

"You missed your family."

"Course I did. Didn't want to sleep in her room, having to leave when Mr. Milford come to do his business on her." She pulled the sandwich out of the fire.

"Sounds less harsh than some experiences I've heard of."

She brought the poker to the table and pulled off her toasted creation, then held the poker within a hair's breadth of his chest. His heart pounded and threatened to come out of his chest. "Only somebody who ain't been with the Milfords would say something like that."

Realie walked back to the fireplace and plunged the poker back into the coals. He watched her chew on her sandwich, strings of cheese dribbling down her chin. There was welled-up hurt in those large beautiful eyes of hers.

He pulled his eyes from her beauty, wishing he hurt somewhere, anywhere, so that he could know a fraction of her pain.

What a fool he was.

CHAPTER FOUR

Lawyer wasn't nothing but a fool. He didn't know what it was to be a thing. Up here, riding off in the woods, he didn't have to worry about no one coming after him.

Realie didn't say nothing to the fancy man, even though he kept looking at her like she was one of Milly's lemon cream biscuit sandwiches. Her most favorite thing. Milly'd let her have some. Sometimes. Well, once a year. Her birthday. Her last one, she was twenty-one—just two months ago.

Oh yes, she had a good ole slave life. Shouldn't expect no more than that. Except she did. When she'd turned eighteen and Milly had first brought her a lemon cream biscuit, Milly had jumped and clapped her hands like a child. "May you have many more," she'd said.

More what? The thought had clouded her mind these months since her last lemon cream biscuit two months ago. More of serving? More of sleeping on her hard floor? More of emptying Milly's nasty chamber pot? Far as Realie could see, that's all she would ever have. Why would she want more?

Mr. Milford had told his wife, "You can't treat them so nice. If you're too nice, they'll want too many nice things. Things we can't afford."

"It's just the basics. A cookie never hurt."

"Some things are for us, and some things are for them."

"Foolishness."

"Maybe to you."

"I don't see why we can't let them go and pay them. That's how we do it in New York."

"New York isn't Georgia, my dear. There would be rioting here if we did that."

She'd easily heard the conversation since the Milfords thought little more of her than they did of their cabbage rose carpet. Her ears had rung and her fingers tingled with the thought of having lemon cream biscuits every day, not just the three she'd had in her life.

And if a man came into her life?

Well, several of them had. She had slapped hands away from her body more times than she could count. Even gave in a couple a times. But there wasn't anything special about it for her.

"You must keep yourself pure, Aurelia," Milly had insisted when she laid out her clothes one morning.

Realie had wanted to laugh in her face. "Why?"

Milly couldn't answer her. She was a fool too.

Realie knew why. If she got a big belly like her mother, she would be weighed down by it. Wouldn't be able to jump up as quick in the night to run some fool errand for Milly with a baby in her belly. Then she would have to take care of the baby and her attention would be split from Milly. Oh no. Have to keep yourself pure.

Milly didn't have to worry. Realie didn't want no baby neither. Especially not a girl baby. A baby would come and be a slave. That would be the worst thing. To be like her. Or Mama or any of her sisters. No.

Please, dear Lord, let Mama have a boy baby.

Still, Milly couldn't tell Realie that if she was itching she couldn't scratch. A longing in her body was hers and she would do as she pleased. Just like relieving herself in the pot.

Lawyer's eyes were on her. Had she been all wrong about him when he turned her down?

She didn't need no fancy man to tell her what to do either. If she could just get on to Canada.

Only Lawyer stood in her way.

"I've got to leave again this morning. I'll tell Mrs. Taylor to leave you here."

"Oh my. You want me to stay up in this hot room again?"

Lawyer gathered up the plates. He was the funniest man, doing for himself. Like he didn't understand how it was suppose to be. What was wrong with him? She kinda wanted to laugh inside herself about it, but something stopped her.

He smiled, showing all of those teeth. "You're my wife, aren't you? As such, you need to stay here and prepare for my return."

"If I were your wife, you would take me with you."

Lawyer shook his head. "I'm going to be gone longer this time. Three days. Deeper into the woods. I can't have extra baggage with me."

Perfect. Sounded like time to figure out how to get away.

She'd already tried to unbutton her shift for him. That wasn't going to work since he was so Christian and all. Humph.

"You can't control that horse. She a problem for you. If I was your wife, I would be going with you."

His shoulders went down and she could see he had given up. Sweet baby in the manger. He said, "I'll have to get Mrs. Taylor to pack extra food for you. You'll need a bedroll."

Realie laughed. "You see me with a bedroll coming up here?"

"I suppose that's true." A shadow crossed his face, and she wished she hadn't laughed. What was he so sad about? "You have no dress."

"I put on my old clothes."

"I'm sure Mrs. Taylor has something I can purchase for you to wear."

This man was so fancy. Why? What was the purpose in it? "She cleaned up my clothes. I just sew up the holes you put in it with your gun."

"Those were men's clothes."

"They belong to my brother Simon."

Lawyer waved a hand. "Ok, Simon's clothes. See. They aren't yours. You need women's clothes."

"I don't care." Her fingers slipped up against each other. How would she escape into the woods in women's clothes?

"Well, I do. I don't want my wife going around in men's clothes."

Realie shook her head. "You forgetting. I'm not your wife, man."

Lawyer folded his arms. "You're here under my protection because I said you were my wife." He matched her shaking head. "I don't like to lie, but there is a greater good involved here that God knows about. It's not right for you to be enslaved, no matter how nice your mistress tried to be. And I'm going to do something about it. I have to finish this loop on the circuit. Then we'll go back to Oberlin, and I'll talk to Charles Henry about what to do."

She folded her hands to stop them from shaking. "Who he?" Nobody else needed to know about her.

"He's my mentor. Kind of like a father figure. He'll help me decide what to do."

"You ask him stuff all the time?"

"Yes. I trust him. I wouldn't be a lawyer without him."

"He have a white skin?"

"He does."

Goodness, Lawyer was a fool. She wasn't trusting a one of them.

For now, she had no choice, so she would play sweet. "If we had time, I could make my own dress."

"We don't. I've got to get on the road in a few hours. So I'll ask Mrs. Taylor and we'll do our best. Excuse me."

He stepped from the room with the breakfast tray and Realie wished she could run. Sometimes it was better to bide time. She'd learned that from her older brothers. She would play along nice with him. Wouldn't hurt for now.

Still, Lawyer was a nice man. Too bad he was a fool. She couldn't afford a fool's choice just now. Too costly.

When Lawyer came back, he carried an old patched-up brown skirt on his arm. "She sold me this. You might have to make do with the shirt you got. She gave me a needle and some thread if you need to fix things."

Looked like the skirt Mrs. Taylor wore to muck out the stables. "It'll do. You get to setting things up and I'll get dressed."

He smiled with relief and left the room again. Humph. Fool again.

She shrugged into the skirt, pleased to see that she had to fold it over several times to make it fit. She used the needle and white thread to repair the hole in Simon's shirt and took the skirt in enough times to make it fit. When she put it on, she almost felt human, but her beat-up work shoes, caked with mud, stuck out on her legs. The skirt wasn't long enough to hide them. Nothing she could do about that. She smoothed down her short hair with shaking fingers and it kept springing back up.

No matter. She would only be with Lawyer for a short time, and then she would be off.

For some reason, the realization made her sad. He had been nice to her, taking care of her. If he ever got his nose up out of them books, he would make some woman a nice husband.

The thought made her stomach churn a little bit. Or maybe Mrs. Taylor's cheese wasn't fresh.

Still, such a handsome man, so successful, should find himself a wife. Maybe, back in that Oberlin place, he had him a sweetheart.

Give Lawyer man someone for company in his life. And please help me get to Canada.

Mama always said to ask God so he could hear your prayers, but it seemed to Realie as if God didn't hear Mama's prayers. And her prayers were special. So Realie didn't think she was heard either.

Except this time. Maybe it would be okay this time. Praying was like skipping stones across the pond. Sometimes it made it across, sometimes no. Got to try, though.

Nice enough for him. But Realie was not going back to no Oberlin. She was going on up to Canada.

Still, when she came down the steps in Mrs. Taylor's patched-up skirt, which probably looked better than it had in years, Realie's fingers tingled like a lemon biscuit was in her grasp. She was so glad to be leaving this tavern. It wasn't no kind of home to her, just a place to stop over.

Time to be moving on.

CHAPTER FIVE

The horse still wouldn't obey.

Realie stepped up to him and held her hand out. Bridgewater sniffed her hand and she petted his nose, crooning in some soft, unfamiliar voice that sounded nothing like the hard, questioning tone he was used to hearing from her. What kind of lady's maid was so in love with horses?

"You work much with horses?" he asked.

She smoothed down the horse's nose, saying something like, "Precious, pretty." Then she looked at him and glared. "She know you questioning her. Can't you see?"

No. He couldn't see. A horse was to get around on, not make friends with. "She rents out to various people. She should be used to constant change."

"Just the way a fool man who puts his nose in books all the time would say." Realie traced a small hand up the horse's neck up to its mane, and with her left arm, swung herself up onto the horse's back.

He couldn't keep his jaw from slacking open. Swung up on the horse, she looked like some goddess from the Amazon—strong, proud, and beautiful.

Now he knew himself as a fool from the city.

"If you're coming, you going to have to get on behind me. I stay in front. She won't like you in the front."

"Miss Realie. I have been the one in the front this entire trip."

She fixed him with a side glance. "That's why you been having trouble, isn't it? She doesn't like you."

The warm feeling crawling up his arms was a clear signal to him. Realie meant *she* didn't like him either.

The warmth in the hot June day made it harder to climb aboard the horse. Or was it that the horse wouldn't be still? He tried twice and felt like a new schoolboy trying to get it right.

He couldn't believe it—he an Oberlin graduate, about to be certified as a lawyer. How could this be happening? "You must hold the horse still."

"I am. You so Christian that you should know she one of God's creatures. Got a mind of her own. She don't want to be still, 'cause you can't even be bothered to know her name. She just want me on her."

"Well then, since you are in the throes of sisterhood, you need to explain to her that I'm the one who needs to be on the horse so I can ride circuit and get back to Oberlin for my exams."

Realie leaned down and whispered some nonsense in the horse's ear. "Try it now."

Lawrence swung up onto the horse with no trouble. Why had the horse stayed still that time?

Because Realie told her to. The young woman could make magic.

Sitting behind her, he could smell her sweat mingled with the woods, an outdoors smell. It was as if he suddenly had a window into her soul. She belonged to the outdoors. Being a lady's maid would have been like stomping on her spirit, and he could see why she ran away from her "kind" slave owners.

He reached around her for the reins, his arms cradling her. The feel of their bodies against each other was a heady sensation. Used to being alone, he hadn't known his heart was hungry and lonely for companionship. Until he lucked into meeting her.

Her voice came cool and smooth. "You expecting to go anywhere?"

"I told you I have to ride the circuit."

"Then you better let me do the steering of the horse. Take your arms from around me."

He did as she asked. "I didn't mean to offend."

"I know. You been doing pretty good up to now, fancy man. That's why I didn't do any jumping. But many a man has many a plan to get what he want. And I'm not for the taking."

He opened his mouth to remind her of how easily she opened her shift to him just a few days ago, then closed it. No point in stirring up trouble. They had some journey ahead of them.

Where to put his arms and hands? She had bunched up her skirt to function as a kind of extra saddle. He put his hands on her hips, and she seemed to mind that less.

He minded. His hands were hovering too close to her rounded backside, and he warmed.

Realie paid no mind to his discomfort. "Going north?"

"Yes. I'll tell you when to alter your path."

Holding onto her, very near to her backside, they went off together, with Lawrence more uncomfortable than he had ever been in his life.

"Right here."

They approached a clearing, and she pulled Berengaria up short. "Here?"

The question in her voice made him look all around. It didn't look like much. But the townspeople knew he would be here the third Thursday of every month to settle disputes, sign off on deeds, and even marry people if necessary. On a sunlit June day, there might more weddings and celebrations today. He hoped so.

His stomach rumbled a bit from the bread and cheese he'd had earlier, but also from nerves at thinking about the examination. They had to let him pass, after all the hard work he'd done. What else would he do with himself? This was all the money he had. Every dime was invested in getting to this point. There was no other outcome for him.

"Stake the horse here, and we'll have some lunch. Spread my bedroll out for us to eat on. They'll be along shortly."

Realie did what he said. It didn't occur to him until after he prayed over the chicken drumsticks, apples, and bread that every word he had spoken to her was a command. He said, "I apologize."

"What you sorry for? Ain't no fault of yours that Mrs. Taylor lady is so mean with her table."

His laugh rang out in the woods. "What gives you cause to say that?"

Realie spread her hands in front of the food on their pseudo table. "She knew I was coming with you. She give you enough for you, not for me too."

"I'm not that hungry."

"You better not be."

He smiled slowly at her. "I guess you're right. However, people will come for courts and weddings and bring food with them. They'll share."

"Did she know that?"

Nodding his head, he thought back. Mrs. Taylor had to. The first circuit stop was at the tavern. She knew.

"Humph. Seem like to me that married lady got a powerful hankering for you, Lawyer. Then you come along and tell her you got a wife. I provide a mighty big excuse for you so she can't grab at you like she want."

"Realie, you are being preposterous. Mrs. Taylor is married."

"You ever see who she's married to?"

His mind flashed to the withered, dried apple core face of Mr. Taylor. "I know. He's an...older gentleman."

"Well, if I had to choose between an old man and a nice young one like you...how old are you, Lawyer?"

"I'm 24, and you do realize you speak of adultery? A sin against God and man."

She tossed the chicken bones into the woods. "You so sure you know God's way that you barely know anything of what humans do. When you going to open your eyes and live?"

Her words took him aback, but fortunately people were beginning to arrive in the clearing. Judging from the large family groups, carrying flowers and banners, he had at least one wedding to perform.

Weddings were typically his favorite part of riding circuit—making man live according to God's law. Realie being with him, pretending to be his wife, made the task harder. Their relationship was a lie.

Still, he had to protect her until he could get back to Oberlin and really help her. He surely didn't want her to return to her previous condition of enslavement.

I'm protecting her.

The job of a husband. When they sheltered in someone's barn for the night, they would be expected to stay together.

He had only been through this area three times, but the settlers were happy to hear he was married. They opened their baskets to share food in celebration. The women gathered about Realie, indulging her. She laughed, took offered plates of food, held babies in her good arm and appeared friendly to all.

Mr. Sampson came to talk to him between marriage ceremonies. "Good thing you got a wife. Riding circuit must be lonely. Looks like you found the right kind of wife." *That I did.*

He gripped at his marriage Bible and gave Mr.Sampson a firm smile. Why would he think such a thing so quickly to himself?

Still, the warmth inside of him at seeing her happy gave him the joy he needed to perform three marriages and oversee punishment for one man who wasn't kind to his wife. He addressed the man, frowning as he passed on judgment. "Remember the word of God. The wife is to her husband as the church is to God. When you understand that, then you understand how to treat your wife. Any other way is living against his word."

He turned away to sign a marriage license for the last couple. When he finished, his eyes wandered over the crowd to see where Realie was. He didn't see her. He and Realie—they were the only people with brown skin, so they would be obvious

He ran to the edge of the clearing but didn't see her. "Has anyone seen my wife?"

Mr. Sampson clapped him on the shoulder. "She must have gone to the privy or something, man. She'll be fine. Don't panic."

Making his way back to the edge and the temporary table to finish signing documents for the happy couple, something gnawed at him, making him want to sit instead of stand, and he couldn't figure out why.

Then it hit him.

Ballentine. The real name of the horse. Ballentine was gone.

"Realie!" Cupping his hands around his lips, he called out for her and ran into the forest. "Ladies, search the privies!"

Everyone stopped celebrating the newest newlywed couple. His boots felt extra snug on him as he ran about, calling her name. But it was as he feared. Realie was gone.

Mr. Sampson laughed. "Dear Lord, did you send her home to her mama already? Ye haven't been married long at all."

The other men joined in as they formed a search party. Only the truth wasn't funny to him. Realie was gone. She didn't trust him to gain her freedom in a legal, more legitimate way. She succeeded in taking his horse and running off to Canada.

What hurt worse? Her lack of trust or that she had run away? Did his pain even matter anymore?

CHAPTER SIX

Demons lived in a place like this. She knew because Mam told her so. In slave church, they always told stories about a dark pit just like this forest. It was the middle of the day, but the forest was so thick, so dense with trees, that it seemed like the sun went back home. How could that be?

She had made it through many forests like this getting up here—why was she thinking of this now? Cause she was so close?

She'd thought taking the horse would get her to Canada faster. That wasn't true, though. She'd been just as much of a fool as Lawyer. She was going slow. Too slow.

Fancy lawyer man would be on her before she knew it.

She gripped the beautiful horse's reins tighter to rid her fingers of the tingly feeling they got whenever she thought of him. Was this the same woods they went through before? How come she hadn't noticed? Was she so busy being in the lead, feeling his strong body behind her, that she didn't know?

That's why she'd told him to get his arms from 'round her. Made her feel all dizzy up in her head. Had to keep her senses to know which direction was which. She thought she had done that. The disappointment in herself got her to biting on her lips like she was hungry—but she wasn't—they had all that food back at the clearing.

Pretty horse wasn't going to know. Realie kept looking for the moss on the trees like her brothers told her and she wasn't seeing any. So she didn't know if the pretty horse was not headed north. Hard to know, though, which way was north in these dark woods. She sniffed, trying to smell the air for that fish smell of the lake, but it didn't come into the forest.

She leaned over to pet the horse. "You going back to the tavern? Back to what you know? Smart thing."

Maybe it was. If she went back to the tavern and then went north, Lawyer wouldn't find her. His good sense and smarts would draw him north to Canada.

Still, it gave her a bad feeling in her stomach to draw Lawyer off like that. He was a kind man, only trying to help her out. Her mother would shake a finger at her.

Was God against her too? She spoke out into the forest. "Except you ain't never been for me, no way, no how. Slaving for Milly Milford. It ain't right, God. I do better."

She reached into her sack and pulled out some of the goods she'd wrapped up in napkins. The folks in that clearing sure were nice. Couldn't believe it. If she had ever thought people would treat her so kindly, give her apple fritters like she was chewing on now, she might have run away a long time back. Too bad Mam didn't know about how kind some could be.

What was Mam doing right now? Who knew? Maybe even slaving for Milly Milford herself? A sudden sting of tears came to Realie's eyes. She hoped not. Mam was too heavy with child. She shouldn't be doing that. Still, them Milfords kept her busy, caring for the other slave children and sewing all day. She could whip up anything. When Milly found out about Mam's sewing talent, she kept her busy all the time. Called her modes—no—*modeste.* "*Modeste.*" Fancy sounding word lawyer man would know.

Don't think about him.

Better to keep her mind on home. Mam wanted her to get away, wanted her to live her own life. Realie wanted to know what new life her mother was going to bring into the world, but more than that, she wanted to live free of Milly's reach and of emptying her chamber pot. To be outside whenever she wanted and to take care of her own self. Too bad she didn't have her Mam's talent with the needle. Needlework seemed to be Calla's talent, but she could deal with animals. Taming horses had to be worth something to someone.

Calla, her next sister down, probably got to be Milly's maid. She might like it too. That's just how fool Calla could be at times.

Sun broke through the trees. Praise be! The tavern was just up ahead. The horse seemed to pick up her footsteps, but something—she couldn't say what—gave her pause. She gathered the reins tightly so the horse would stop too. Something smelled bad. Trouble. Not the fish from the lake. Something else.

Sure enough, she could see three strange white men with that Mrs. Taylor woman on the porch.

Realie didn't like the look of them. The fat greasy-haired men carried guns. The wind blew their stink in her direction, and she thought she would faint. Sure didn't smell nice like Lawyer.

Mrs. Taylor looked a little too smug underneath her white ruffly day cap. The bad feeling rolled around in Realie's stomach, and she wanted to faint. Those men were slave catchers—had to be. They were there for her. The wind carried Mrs. Taylor's tinny voice.

"I knew he wasn't married to her. Living up in my room in some kind of sin. And to think I thought better of him. Called himself a Christian, but secreting away property in my tavern! Circuit rider or no, he'll never be welcomed here, for sure."

"Any idea where he get off too?"

"His next circuit's over in Allensberry's Grove. It's the longest way away. He saves it for last."

One of the slave catchers peered in her direction. She shrunk back. *Dear God, hide me in these hell trees.* The pretty horse stayed silent, silent as the grave. Smart horse. She knew trouble came out of that stink.

"He coming back here?"

"He might. He sometimes will stay over again, but he took all of his stuff with him this time, so I don't think so."

"We can stay right here 'til he do."

"We need to find him."

"I'm not looking to go into them woods. Looks like the devil's hideout."

Realie shivered. Slave catcher thinking like her. What should she do? Go back to the clearing near the grove with the nice people?

God, I wished I'd more sense and stayed with Lawyer. He said he was going to help me, but I didn't trust him.

She kept blinking faster and faster. No time to go all womanish now. She had to keep going. Go north. Now she could see moss on the trees, and she needed to follow it to Canada.

She slid off the horse and whispered into her ear. "Sorry, sugar. Got to keep on going. Hope I find a nice lake or creek for you to drink out of, but I got to keep going." She reached into the rucksack, found an apple she'd taken from the table, and gave it to the horse, starting to lead her away from the tavern, turning her steps in line with the moss.

Strong arms grabbed her.

The slave catchers! She wasn't going to make it!

Strong arms squeezed hard and a hand covered her mouth. *God, help me.*

The whispering voice in her ear caused her to wilt. "Stay still, Realie. You got us in a heap of trouble here."

Lawyer!

Her heart beat fast for a different reason. Yeah, he smelled much better than them slave catchers.

She stayed still, and the horse did too. Lawyer took his hand from her mouth but didn't release his hold on her. She liked that fine since his arms were nice and warm. Like home was in his arms. "I'm sorry, Lawyer."

"Who those men?"

"I think they're slave catchers. They going to wait at the tavern for you to come back."

He let her go. "Sorry if I pressed on your wound."

She hadn't even noticed until he let her go and the wound started to throb with the beat of her heart.

"Get up on the horse. I'll lead. We've got to get back to Oberlin, soon as we can." Lawyer pulled her up onto the pretty horse. How did he find her so fast?

"Don't they know to look for you there?"

His handsome face looked like the Grim Reaper. They were in deep trouble, sure enough. Because of her. Why had she messed things up?

"They do. But since they're lazy and they're holing up at the tavern—waiting, drinking, and doing God knows what with Mrs. Taylor—we might have a chance to get ahead of them. That's what I'll pray for."

A lot of sense in his plan, but one thing bothered her. "Why you say that about Mrs. Taylor?"

His face made a funny shape, like he smelled something bad. "She's a woman who plies her wares easily, cuckolding her husband and breaking her covenant with God in committing adultery. All that matters to her is money."

"Could be, but she wanted to be with you for free."

"I should think you would be too young to know such things."

"I know a lot of things, Lawyer."

"I suppose you do. Now get up on that horse. And be quiet."

Realie obeyed. For once.

The night started to fall and the woods hemmed them in. She'd thought it was dark before. No, this was much, much worse. They had a ways to go too. She could tell by the hard set of Lawyer's jaw.

Pretty horse was getting tired. They had asked a lot of her today. Where would they stop for the night? And when? She wanted to ask those questions, but her throat was dry.

So she said, "Rucksack empty."

"I know."

His voice shook cause of the mad in him at her. He should be. Her heart sank into the beat-up shoes she wore.

"What we going to do?"

"Hold onto Ballentine's mane. If you get sleepy, I'm sure she'll let you lie down and sleep."

"I'm not tired."

He made some kind of noise, like he thought she was lying. She didn't appreciate that, 'cause she didn't lie. Well, except when he forced her to say she was his wife and such. That was a lie, for sure.

Up ahead, a little cabin sat back from the road. Lawyer led the horse to the door and knocked on it. Realie couldn't see in the darkness, but she heard him talking to somebody.

In a moment he came back. "We can stay in the barn for the night. Mrs. Cole will bring us some food."

Praise God.

He helped her off the horse, and she led pretty horse into the barn. She asked him when he came in after her, "You call this horse Ballentine?"

A small smile crossed his lips. "That's the horse's name. Guess I had to be focused enough to remember. My mind's on many things these days."

He pulled the bedrolls and materials from Ballentine's back and made up a mound of fresh hay away from the horses. "This is the best we can do."

A small woman with brown skin came into the barn with a bag full of food. "It's not hot, Judge, but it's hearty."

"Thank you, Thunder. I appreciate it."

"Since when you get a woman?"

"She's not mine, Thunder. Don't start things."

The woman smiled, showing teeth through the darkness, and Realie's heart sank at Lawyer's declaration that she was none of his. Prickles dotted her skin. Why should she care what he said? She would be free in Canada soon, not belonging to any man.

"I just know your grandmother would want to know these things, if she was."

His face got all serious again. "You see her recently?"

"No. Maybe I'll go near autumn. But that's not saying you can't go visit."

"I know. I've been busy. I'll make time. Thanks to you and John for letting us stay out here."

"Least I can do."

The woman slipped away, and Realie helped Lawyer lay out the bedrolls on the soft hay. They opened the bag and found a warmish meat pie of some kind and apples.

Realie knew not to say anything to him as they ate. When he finished, she gave his core and the rest of her apple to Ballentine. "Who is that woman? She Indian?"

"Yes. A distant cousin of mine, most likely. She's of the People."

What did that mean? "She family but didn't want you inside?"

"Her husband's white. We could have gone inside, but I'm not sure I trust him to not report you. I offered to stay out here."

"I see." She cleaned up the eating space and stretched out on the bedroll. The hay was nice and soft. Almost as good as the tavern bed. His bedroll was next to hers, and he stretched out too. Right beside her.

"I'm sorry I got you in this trouble, Lawyer. I didn't know."

He turned over. "Just get some rest. God'll provide for us. Pray. We need to believe in his faithfulness."

The words shattered her inside, and she felt like grabbing her arm in frustration. He was still mad at her. How could he? He had shot her, after all. The hurt throbbed in her arm, but she turned over on her good side and tried to sleep.

Sometime in the night though, he pulled her to him, and his chest made the perfect pillow for her to rest her head on. His arms were the best blanket. This was what it meant to be close to someone.

Chapter Seven

One thing about Realie, she was a sturdy traveler. A good quality for a circuit court judge's wife.

What made him think that?

He shook his head to clear the fuzz out of it. They had left the Coles' barn just before dawn and now, around the midpoint of the day, were in Oberlin. The city was quiet this Sunday morning, which was what he needed to slip Realie into his room at the boarding house so he could go to Charles Henry and see what could be done about her. Then he'd get her a room of her own. He didn't want anyone making the mistake here that she was his wife.

He and Ballentine bounced gently, because Realie slept on with her arm sticking out. Hopefully, there was no infection growing in there, but he had to get her to a real doctor, one he trusted, who could examine her and help her heal. His mentor would know which doctor would help.

Thank you, God, for Oberlin. He was proud that his adopted city and college town abhorred slavery and its by-products.

He warmed as he regarded her sleeping form and her poor attempt to look like a man. It would be nice to have someone to arrange his meals for him, see to him when he was done for the day, have someone to talk to so he wouldn't be lonely.

A wife.

Although this was the time of day on a Sunday when he normally made his way to First Christian Church, he took a side road to Charles Henry's office. Charles lived in a white, wooden board townhouse next door. Lawrence left the sleeping Realie on the horse, went up the front steps, and knocked on the door. Anna Henry, a large jolly woman dressed in her finest Sunday clothing, opened the door. "What're you doing here, Lawrence? I thought you were riding circuit."

"I—I got into a bit of a situation, and I had to come back. I'll ride back to Allensberry's Grove and finish the circuit."

"What happened?" Anna looked behind him and saw Realie sleeping on Ballentine.

"She's a runaway. She's been shot." There was no time to mince words on the open street. Anna would understand.

Her eyes slid sideways in both directions. "Bring her in. Now." Yes, many people in Oberlin were abolitionists, but harboring Realie was still breaking the law.

Lawrence plucked her off the horse and held her close. Her body felt too warm.

Anna pointed him to a small room behind the kitchen where there was a bed. "Let her lie down there. I'll tell Charles to send for the doctor."

"Will the doctor treat her?"

Anna waved his concerns away. "My goodness. We're always coming up against this situation." She fixed him with a direct look. "We're a way station, you know."

Lawrence nodded. He had always assumed so, with the way that Charles spoke, but he didn't want to pry. Some knowledge had not been worth having.

Anna gazed at Realie. "She's a pretty girl."

He nodded again. "She's sure a handful. A lot for any man to deal with."

"Maybe she's someone who could care for you."

"Me? I can barely take care of myself."

Anna led them out of the little room and closed the door. "Which is why you need someone to take care of you."

"She just left enslavement. Would it be right to resign her to marriage? Something like enslavement?"

Anna pursed her lips and straightened up her bulk to face him. "I am Charles's equal in every way in this house."

"It's just outside the house when that changes."

"It can be different for you."

He doubted it. He opened his mouth to say more when his mentor joined them. Anna escorted them into the parlor and she quickly related who Realie was.

"Of course we'll help her," Charles said. "But she's been shot? Doesn't sound as if she's law-abiding."

"I shot her." They both turned to him, amazed. He shrugged his shoulders. "Well, she was trying to steal Ballentine."

He folded his arms and gave them a half smile, glad to fill them in on the rest of his adventure.

Charles Henry shook his head. "I'm going by your word here, Lawrence. I know and trust you. If she's intent on going to Canada, we better help her do that. Sounds as if she's pretty determined."

"We've got to go to services." Anna stood. "There's bread and cold chicken in the kitchen. You are more than welcome to stay and tend to her. As a matter of fact, I would prefer that you would." He could take advantage of some study in Charles's library while Realie healed.

"She's really harmless." His heart stung at how his friends perceived Realie. Then again, why should he care at all?

But he did. "Please make my apologies at church. I'll stay here."

Charles held his wife's hand. "Fine. We'll bring the doctor back with us. We'll figure out how to get her across the border when we return."

He wanted to agree.

No. It was too hard to form the words to help Realie go away from him.

After they left, he knelt. *Help me to decide what is best for Realie.*

He sat down in Charles Henry's spacious library and did some hard studying, something he hadn't accomplished in months. It felt good to dig back into the texts again, but as he read a tort about property, a piercing screech rang through the house.

Realie!

He ran to her side. Her body was enveloped in a full sweat. He hurried to the kitchen and pumped water into a basin and grabbed a rag. By the time he returned, Realie was flat on the bed again and quiet. He bathed her limbs gently, in prayer. *What should I do about her, Lord? What can be done?*

The answer came clearly as he cleansed the area around her wound, taking care to keep her dressing dry. She moaned in pain through her sleep and stabbed him through his worry.

Free her.

He was a poor almost-lawyer, so low on the chain of being, as it were, but if her freedom meant so much to her, he would drive himself into debt. He would help her by freeing her. She could stay here in the United States and be free. What did she know about Canada, a foreign land? She could even stay in Oberlin. If the owners of the livery stable could see how she was with the horses, she might get a job. He would ask around.

The pain at losing her eased in his heart, and he dropped the rag in joy when the sound of the front door opening reached him and voices echoed throughout the house. The Henrys entered the room with a doctor in tow, concerned looks on their faces. Someone was here; someone qualified to help her.

Thank you, God.

After dinner, Charles Henry beckoned Lawrence into his library.

He looked over his shoulder toward the small room where Realie rested.

Anna waved a hand at him. "You go ahead. You've been watching over her all day long. If she calls for you, I'll come and get you."

"Thank you, ma'am."

He seated himself in one big, comfy chair while Charles went around to the other chair and sat down, watching the carriages go by in the early summer evening.

"You all studied up for the exams?"

It was not in his heart to lie. "It's been harder over the past few days, riding circuit and all."

Charles shook his head. "Don't blame the circuit. I got more done when I used to ride, since I was alone. Until Anna came along and begged me to take her with me."

"More people are moving out here and making towns. Maybe circuit riding is a thing of the past."

"Could be. Passing your exams would help, but you don't exactly need them."

"A man with brown skin needs proof of his worth."

"I believe you. But that girl, she's causing you to be distracted."

"Some. I've got to help her, though. God put her in my life."

"I don't disagree. God has also provided a way to help her on. We'll take care of that, so you can get back to your studying."

Lawrence shook his head. "I don't think that's what she wants."

His friend made a loud sound, and the tips of his ears burned red. "What do you know of what she wants? She was willing to commit a hanging offense to get away."

"That's when she thought that was her only choice. If she could find a job, then she'd probably prefer to stay in the boarding house."

"The slave catchers will find her some day."

"Not if she's free."

"Only way to free her is to buy her."

"Exactly. I'll buy her."

"You don't have two buffalo nickels to rub together, Lawrence. Mind like a steel trap but you got nothing."

"You do."

The silence fell between them. Had he made a mistake viewing Charles Henry as a friend rather than as a white man? Everything Lawrence had become had been because of this man before him, someone he'd viewed as an intelligent man. But was he a compassionate one too?

"You'll be in debt to me for some time. You say she's a lady's maid? They won't let her go for no less than eight hundred dollars, a thousand at the most."

Dry cotton invaded his mouth. *Dear God.*

"Oh yes. Those slave owners want their comforts. They don't want to do for themselves. That's why slavery is so popular."

"You know a great deal about it."

"I've made it my business to study them. Have to study the enemy you know. They purposefully avoid their own labor, in clear abeyance of what God said to Adam and Eve before he cast them from the Garden of Eden. It's dangerous."

"I don't mind."

"Fine. I'll forward you extra money for your steamboat fare and a new set of clothes. You must go looking your very best. Go as a Miami if you need to—they are bound to respect that more. Promise me that you will stay in your stateroom on the boat. Study. Do not come out. Have meals brought to you. Be satisfied to be a mystery to the other passengers. Only under these circumstances will I loan you the money."

"Very well." Lawrence went to him to shake his hand. Charles gave him a wry smile. "You are willing to go into the mouth of hell to help this young woman."

"It's the right thing to do, sir."

"I hope she's worth it."

"She's God's child. It makes her worth it. Thank you. I'm going to go check on her."

"I hope she's there when you do." The chuckles of Charles Henry chased him out of the library and down the hallway as he entered the kitchen.

Anna folded a dishrag clearly finished with. "I thought I heard her stirring in there. Here's a cup of the beef broth the doctor wants her to have. You feed it to her."

Lawrence took the cup. "Thank you."

"You're welcome. Good luck now."

He opened the door and Realie looked at him, her long lashes sweeping her cheeks. She smiled, and two pretty dimples dented her skin.

He stopped in his tracks, stunned. Those were new. The dimples framed her face, as beautiful as the dawn. Yes, he would march into the pit of hell for her. He would do anything for that face and those dimples. Not so she would be grateful to him, but so she would know how much and how deeply she had invaded his heart, the one he had protected so long hiding himself away in his studies.

CHAPTER EIGHT

These people Lawyer left her with were too nice, so Realie knew she couldn't trust them. No, she had grown up with the wrong people for too long—like Milly saying she would do one thing for her and then never doing it. Never referring to it. Dangling a lemon cream biscuit over her as if it were a carrot for Ballentine.

No matter what Lawyer said before he left, she still couldn't trust it.

Dear Lord, heal me up. I got to get out of here.

Canada still called to her. All that time, she heard the sweet sound of the word in her ears, but now... Lawyer was on his way to the Milford place to buy up her freedom. Why would he do that? A small stirring in her belly made her feel like it would be wrong to leave just now.

She didn't want him down there, but then he could tell Mam she was safe. That she'd made it to freedom.

Still, part of her was afraid he would never come back, or that everything these people had told her was a lie. He might even be sold into slavery himself.

"Poor dear," the lady kept saying as if she weren't in the room, handing her some old dresses to fix up for wearing,

"She doesn't know who to trust. What an aberration slavery can be."

Still, the man—she could see right off he didn't trust her. "Lock all the doors. She might steal the silver to sell."

"The poor child doesn't know her way around town, Charles. How would she know where to sell any silver?"

"She could find out. She's bright, that one. How did she make that impossible journey up here? Not as smart as Lawrence with his mixed blood, but still smart."

Dear Lord, why did they talk about her right there in the kitchen as if she couldn't hear through her door? Why did they have to be transparent?

We can see through their skins, see through their minds and into their hearts. Mam always used to say that, and she was right.

So she kept an eye on them and on her scar, making sure it healed right. It was fixing, but she didn't have a friend in the world. She hated sewing, but fixing the old dresses helped the time pass. She didn't have Mam's talent, but she worked on it. She only had that terrible rag thing that Mrs. Taylor from the tavern gave her. She wanted to look nice when Lawyer came back with her freedom papers.

She wanted to look like she was worthy of freedom.

A few days after Lawyer left, Realie got out of bed and went into the kitchen. Her fixed up skirt was crooked, but at least it wasn't that terrible rag from the tavern lady. She wanted to burn that thing.

"You're up bright and early," the lady said to her.

"I can work for my keep, ma'am. Had enough lying around."

"My goodness. Do you know how to cook?"

She'd never had to bother, so she shook her head. "I can learn, ma'am."

"Peel these potatoes." Miss Lady handed her a knife and a bag of potatoes.

Realie got down to work and peeled six of them until Miss Lady told her to stop.

"You didn't do much cooking as a slave, did you?"

"No. I was in the house serving Miss Milly. I can do hair and iron up clothes to make them look nice. And take care of horses, but that's cause I like them."

"I've heard." The lady's smile was kind.

"I can do that for you, if need be."

"We have other servants to take care of the horses, dear, but thank you. Right now, you need to learn how to cook something, at least a stew if you're going to take care of Lawrence."

Lawyer didn't care nothing about her like that. "What do you mean, ma'am?"

"My dear, I've never seen Lawrence have a tender affection for anyone before. He's quite taken with you."

"You fooling me for sure, Missus. I never said nothing."

"You didn't have to, dear. He's a young man. Lonelier than he would care to admit. He needs a woman, someone to care for him. I've been praying that someone could be you. And it would give me great pleasure to teach Lawrence's wife how to care for him."

"If you don't mind me asking, ma'am, how you get to know him?"

The good lady wiped her hands on her apron. "Charles and I were never blessed with children of our own. It's the reason Charles was able to loan him money to procure your freedom."

Realie looked away from the peas she snapped.

"We've always had extra. His grandmother, a full-bloodied Miami, always had him in tow when she came into town. His mother died when he was young, I understand. He was so intriguing, a pretty brown child. Longest eyelashes in the world. We talked her into letting him come to town for school. He did so well. He was so bright. You can't help but be naturally drawn to a child like that."

"Who his daddy be?"

"His grandmother didn't know. She thinks he was an escaped slave somehow. But that's the reason he's a freeman. Always has been. When his grandmother and the rest of the Miami were ordered to leave, she wanted him to stay and be educated. We took him in as our ward, but once he grew up and graduated from Oberlin, he wanted to move out on his own. He's always been independent."

Miss Lady turned to Realie. "But equally important, he sees his being here as ordained by God. He was fashioned by our maker to help his people. He needs a helpmate to do that work. Is that you?"

Realie smiled. "I'm sure they's plenty of pretty ladies been to school and church up here to be with him."

To her surprise, the lady put down the carrot she was dealing with and grasped Realie's hands. "Slavery's taught you that you aren't worthy of God's love."

"Oh, I believe in God, ma'am. I just don't know if he believes in me."

The woman squeezed her hands. "We'll have to pray on it. Pray you through."

A nice idea, but Realie didn't know how well it would work. Still, as her wound healed and the days and weeks ticked by, she grew more worried about Lawrence. Was he all right? Was he able to buy her? Would Milly let her have her freedom? What would Mam say? Would he have a chance to talk to her?

She hoped so.

She wondered about Ballentine, longing to see her. But the couple kept her penned up in the house, and the husband always looked strangely at her, telling her, "You are collateral against my loan to Lawrence. You must stay here."

The wife would open her mouth real wide at his talk. Realie wasn't surprised, though. That's how people would be sometimes. She wasn't anything more than an end table to him.

"She is entitled to breathe free, husband. It's what we are working for."

"You go with her then. Anyone who would steal a horse would easily steal herself."

One day Anna untied her apron, tilted the lid on the stew pot and faced her. "I trust you, dear. Go to the livery stables and have a good visit with the horse. Come back in an hour. Do you know long that is?"

Realie gathered it wasn't too terribly long.

Still, as she walked the streets of Oberlin with nothing on her but apples and carrots in her pockets for the horse, she wanted to whirl to invisible music. This must be what freedom was like.

She could run away—she didn't like the way the husband looked at her. More important, she wanted to be here to talk to Lawyer when he got back from down south. See if what Miss Lady said about his feelings was true.

The livery stable man looked at her strange too, but he probably didn't care. She fed Ballentine for free.

Realie slipped her hands around the horse's neck and smelled her hay-scented mane. "Pretty horse. You going to be all right."

Ballentine's rubbery lips scraped her hand as she fed her vegetables and the two apples. She still hated her friend had to stay somewhere where she wasn't loved—just like Realie. She was getting her freedom, but she sure wished Ballentine would get hers too.

She patted the horse down and brushed her for the liveryman. He didn't pay Ballentine no attention, she could tell. "I be back to visit. You be good for the person who gets you next."

The liveryman fixed her with a look. "You a slave?"

"No." Realie stuck her chin out. At least she hoped she wasn't.

"You come on by when you want to brush down the horse."

"Thank you, mister."

"Name's Josiah. You be helping me out. You brush her down real good. The others might need it too."

Praise God. "I'll be back tomorrow, sir." Mr. Josiah didn't need to know about her being bored up at the Henry house. They might be friends, for all she knew. People couldn't be trusted.

Good thing the Henrys didn't live far at all, just down the street aways and around the corner. Oberlin was a real town with several stores, much better than Crumpton near where she'd lived. It wasn't as big as a full city she'd seen making her way up to freedom, like Washington, D.C., all muddy and cloudy. No. Oberlin was a town where a young woman could visit a horse and buy a ribbon or a new dress of her own. Maybe one day.

She stopped on the wooden sidewalk for a minute, thinking to herself, trying to get a handle on her thoughts. If she wasn't a slave no more, she would need money to live. Would Mr. Josiah pay her to take care of the horses?

She had to find out. She turned around to go back to the livery and found a weight pressing on her arm where she was still healing from the gunshot wound. The pain made her want to fall to her knees in pain.

"You come with us, girl."

She screamed, but another man covered her mouth and silenced her. The stinky slave catchers from the tavern. Fear shot through her like snake venom, and her knees sagged. Wasn't there anyone around to help her? No, everyone was inside eating dinner.

"Stop struggling, or we going to make this real unpleasant for you."

She bit the hand over her mouth, and the man yelped. He swung a hand to her cheek and punched her.

Everything blacked out for a moment.

Almost instantly, someone wrapped a rope about her arms and legs and set her on the back of a horse.

Ballentine. They had rented her out after she left.

Tears came to her eyes as the stinky man held her fast on her horse. Well, at least she and her friend would be together on the journey.

Didn't matter what Lawyer did with his pretty teeth and smooth ways. She was on her way back to slavery.

Please God—

She stopped herself. If God cared about her, this wouldn't be happening. She'd tried to tell Miss Lady that God didn't care, and now here was the proof. Miss Lady's husband would be right when Realie didn't come back.

Lawyer would be in debt to the man. For nothing. And she would never see him or his pretty teeth or silky hair or the snug fitting buckskins anymore.

I hope you find a nice lady to take care of you. One you deserves.

Chapter Nine

The weeks that ticked off in the meantime were more than enough time to study. Taking the train from Cincinnati back east to New York and then boarding a steamship that hugged the Eastern Seaboard down south to Georgia, he was free to do as Charles Henry directed him to do. However, he couldn't help but notice that his entire being, his way of existing in the world, had changed. Realie wasn't by his side, and he honestly missed her.

He missed her teasing tone calling him Lawyer, as if he were one—almost as if she believed he'd become one when he hardly believed it himself.

The least he could do was to free her in return. It was part of what he was born to do.

The words of his grandmother, with her full Miami blood, haunted him as he stayed clear of the company on the steamboat and immersed himself in his studies. "You know in your heart what is right and what is wrong. The deep-brown man hasn't been here as long as the People. The white man brought them over to work, and they did what the white man asked, hoping for freedom. When they tried the same with us, they couldn't succeed. Not because we were better, but because we knew the land. So we have to help however we can."

Without even knowing the brown fur trapper who had kept his mother as a wife for a short time and disappeared, Lawrence knew that part of the call in his blood was about helping the enslaved of this country to be free. The Miami were forced to move far away from their home, but the point his grandmother made haunted him—at least they were free.

Realie's smooth, pretty brown skin made him ache with longing to touch her. He had held off though. She had to become his in proper Christian ceremony. After proposing marriage, of course. Maybe he could propose—once he had given her the freedom papers. But he didn't want her to feel obligated. That wouldn't be freedom. It would be like changing one cage for another.

No more cages for Realie.

When the steamboat docked upriver at the Milford plantation, it was early July, and he could barely draw breath through the heavy, wet air. Even so, it was easy to see how prosperous the land was, covered in blooming, white flowers. The red fields stretched as far as the eye could see.

When he disembarked, a man unloading the cargo looked at him in shock. "What you doing here?"

He doffed his beaver hat. He had done as Charles directed and dressed in his very best apparel, despite the heat. This man had probably never seen anyone of his race dressed up like him. "I have an appointment with Mr. Franklin Milford."

"With what?"

"Regarding one of his slaves who escaped."

"You talking about Realie?"

Lawrence nodded his head.

"What about her?"

Well, he certainly hadn't expected interrogation today, but he knew that his appearance must be a shock to this man. "I've come to free her."

A large grin split his face. "You mean she made it?"

Better a smile than a frown. He must be on the right track. Lawrence reached out to shake the man's hand, and the man grasped his hand and pumped it up and down. "Praise God. Deliverance come for her. I can ride you to the Milfords in the wagon. You okay swinging up next to me?"

He certainly was. "Had to travel some that way coming down. Let's go."

"I'm Noah. I'm Realie's older brother."

"Nice to meet you." He gave his name and shook the man's hand, looking for a trace of resemblance in his face but found none to Realie.

He swung his case onto the back of the wagon, and Noah watched him. "You can carry your own for a fancy dressed man."

His heart quickened to think of her once more. "You sound a lot like your sister. That's how she thought of me."

"How she doing?"

"Last I left her, she was learning how to live in our community in Ohio. Recuperating, though."

He quickly explained. Noah shouldn't have a moment's concern about his sister. He probably had enough to deal with. They fell into a quiet Lawrence felt compelled to break to be companionable.

"This is beautiful land."

"Sure is. Once you come to Milford, you never want to leave."

"Well, once I process your sister's freedom, I'll be looking to leave."

"But you be back. Some way. That's how it is here."

Not wanting to dispute the man, he looked all around. To the right on the horizon, a slightly ramshackle house appeared. It wasn't pretty, but purposeful. Made of white wood, it was two levels. If it were brick, it would be sturdier. Noah steered into a large open yard in front of the house where an older white woman sat in a chair on the porch. She stood, no doubt startled to see a dressed-up Negro man come to her doorstep.

Be deferential.

He would, but not at the expense of his dignity. Dignity was a terrible cost of slavery, but he was no slave, so he wouldn't pay it.

He nodded to her. "I'm Lawrence Stewart, Esquire, here to conduct business on behalf of Charles Henry regarding one of your runaway slaves."

"You talking about Realie?" The woman wrapped a shawl around her shoulders, even in the deep heat of July.

"Yes. Is your husband available?"

"He is. Come this way."

Only when he jumped down from the wagon did he see that other people, some who resembled Realie, began to gather around. A cluster of young women looked at him, pointing. He nodded, as was polite, and they scattered. With nineteen in her family some of them had to be Realie's younger sisters.

He went up the rickety front stairs, and the woman fixed him with an arched eyebrow. "Wipe your feet out here."

He did as she directed and followed the woman into the house. He gripped lightly at the rim of his hat, noting that the place wasn't as beautiful or stately as he'd expected. They would want to deal with him.

She called out to her husband as they walked through the best decorated room in the house, the parlor, and came to an office. "Franklin. This man has some knowledge of Realie."

An older man with a brown and gray beard turned from his desk and fixed Lawrence with a look. "Well, I'll be. Where do you come from?"

"Ohio. I'm representing the interests of Judge Charles Henry." Lawrence reached into his suit pocket and presented papers.

The man held up a hand. "Why did he send you down here?"

What difference did that make? He kept his voice level. "He doesn't travel as often these days, due to a painful case of the gout. I'm his assistant. I ride circuit for him as well."

"I'll be. And you know Realie?"

"I do."

The woman rushed forward, her blue eyes blazing. "She needs to pay, Frank."

"Milly. Hush. Have a seat, Mr. Stewart—is that correct?"

"It is."

He sat on a couch while the woman kept standing. "I find your timing interesting. I've had word from the catchers I hired. They've found her."

His heart leaped in his throat. "What do you mean, sir?"

"Am I not speaking clearly enough for you? They're bringing her back."

How was that possible? She'd been cooking in Anna Henry's kitchen when he'd left her.

Dear God.

Had he gotten here too late to free her?

He tried not to betray an emotion either way. "Well, that is interesting news." Franklin Milford appeared to be shrewd. He had better be to navigate ownership of a great tract of land like this.

"Praise Jesus, they did their jobs." The woman clasped her hands.

Lawrence refrained from looking at her, but her tone of joy was clear enough. Why should it matter to this woman who served her?

"When she gets back here, she better know her place." The woman's voice sounded harsh, but she didn't sound Southern. Why not?

"Hold on, Milly. This man brings an interesting solution from his judge boss. He gives me money, and I'm rid of a problem."

Lawrence interrupted, "Realie is no problem, sir."

They kept talking to one another as if he weren't there.

"You're here pining for her, asking where she is. I got you another girl, and I still have my silence broken, having to hear about some maid. I will have my quiet, Millicent!"

The woman sat down. One of her braids broke free, and she appeared a petulant child. "I don't mean to disturb you, Mr. Milford, but I just—"

"The house is your territory. I don't know how many times I got to tell you."

"Well, don't blame me, sir. Just because I'm late come to being a wife."

"We've been married for nigh on fifteen years, and you still having a hard time."

"Do you forget, sir, that I'm new to having slaves as well?"

"You never let me, Milly." Franklin Milford lowered his head, shaking it.

He turned himself to address Lawrence, dismissing his marital spat. "Having these slaves is supposed to make life easier, and yet it causes constant conflict between me and my wife."

"There's a price to be paid when you marry for money." The words on Mrs. Milford's breath were so softly spoken, Lawrence believed Mr. Milford couldn't hear it. But given the look on the man's face, he must have known what his wife said.

He would feel sympathy with Franklin Milford—if he didn't hold the care of Realie and her family in his hands. The words of Jesus on the cross rolled through his mind. *Forgive them, Father, for they know not what they do.*

Would to God he could free all of Realie's family.

"It is a very expensive proposition to be a simple cotton farmer, Milly, for that's all I am."

"Clearly." His wife huffed.

"Will you leave me to my business, wife?"

"I will not. I'm staying right here. I know what you plan to do. You're going to sell her to this fancy-dressed Negro, and I won't have it."

"Milly, I have to pay these slave catchers when they bring her here. I don't have the money. This man brings the answer."

"If only you hadn't tied up all of my money in the land."

"That's where the wealth is, my love. And in the slaves. I'm tired of pursuing this young girl. Let her be gone from us so we won't fight anymore. Calla will be used to her new duties soon enough. Give her time."

Mrs. Milford smoothed her frayed hair. "If you don't let Realie know who is boss, she'll be an example to the rest of them to run off. And then what?"

Franklin shook his head. "I doubt that will happen. Many of them don't have the sense Realie does."

"She's kin to most of them. They'll do as she does."

Mrs. Milford's voice became a roughened growl, an interesting slip from her ladylike exterior. Keeping hold of the chains that bound another person was a terrible thing.

"They won't. I'm selling her. We can have my lawyer journey here to finish the papers. Will that do?"

Lawrence wanted to breathe out his relief at it being this easy. Good thing Realie was so hard to pin down. Except that they caught her, and the alarm rose in his throat. *Please let her be alright, Lord.* The image of her smooth brown face rose in his mind, and his heart swelled. He missed her so.

"Mr. Stewart?" Mr. Milford called him out of his thoughts.

"I apologize, Mr. Milford. That's fine with me."

Mrs. Milford huffed. "I do believe Mr. Stewart has some feelings for my Aurelia. Is that so, sir?"

Aurelia? Her real name? How beautiful. He stood to face her. "I wouldn't be telling the truth if I didn't say that Realie has a kind heart and a true spirit that is hard to tame. She's a wonderful example of womanhood."

"She's a slave, sir." Her blue eyes flashed.

Not for much longer, praise God.

"We need to provide hospitality for Mr. Stewart. It will take a day for my lawyer to come, and we must wait for the catchers to bring Realie back. I received word they were in Tennessee, so they should be here within the next week."

"I don't want *Mr.* Stewart in my house."

Lawrence stared at the woman. He would pray for her. Someone like this desperately needed prayer. "I appreciate the thought, Mr. Milford. However, I wouldn't dream of inconveniencing your wife. I'll seek shelter elsewhere."

A slight shadow of embarrassment crossed the man's face, but Lawrence didn't delude himself in thinking that it was about him. No, it was about his wife. "Whatever you prefer, sir. Mr. Stewart?"

Lawrence turned to face the man.

"Is it true that you have an affection for Realie?"

Like a law book slipped off a high shelf, his love for her hit him full in the face. "I do. I have to do the Christian thing by her and court her properly, but I do. She's a rare sort."

A sad smile crossed Franklin Milford's face. "Well then, I wish you all the happiness, sir. Domestic life for a man certainly settles him down."

Yes, he supposed. Especially if a man were married to Milly Milford.

There could be sympathy for Franklin.

Or more empathy. He was in his own form of slavery.

To wait for Realie, Lawrence would not return to Ohio in time for the examination. Instead of a sinking feeling, he felt proud. Walking out of the house, he faced the gathered relatives of Realie with hopeful looks on their faces. His trip to the heart of slavery made him certain he had done the right thing—all because of one woman he lucked upon meeting after she tried to steal his horse.

Praise God.

Chapter Ten

The whole point of this was to make her suffer. That's what she felt like. The times they made her sleep on the hard ground with no blanket were all about suffering.

Kind of like the torment they put the King of Kings through.

She wasn't nobody but some little slave girl on a big old cotton farm.

No, I'm not. I almost made it to Canada. I'ma be proud of that the longest day I live.

No matter what.

The catchers kept fussing between them who was going to get to use her as a bed warmer.

Praise God that it was hot July and that they were traveling on a humid road. It was too humid for them to even want that, not that she was in the business of providing it. No, that part of her was only for Lawyer—if he was to marry her.

"Mr. Milford said don't touch her," one whined to the other.

"What can she say? She won't say nothing. We can do what we like, collect our money, and leave before anyone ever know anything. Old man might even be grateful if we left him behind a little pickaninny present."

The fat one came close, too close. She could smell every part of him—his stink, his sweat, the devil's brew on his breath, and every foul odor from every orifice on him.

Please, God. I needs a miracle now. I need you right by my side today.

Should she have doubted it? Ever? Even in her life as an enslaved handmaid? When he grabbed her breast and tweaked it hard, all of the beans and cornbread they gave her came up in a pungent mess onto his clothes and shoes.

The slave catcher leaped ten feet in the air, and the whiny one laughed and laughed.

He yelled at her and threatened to hit her, but her eyes shone straight on him with the light of God, daring him to hurt her or return her as damaged goods.

He pulled back as if she were fire itself.

All fine and good, but she would keep an eye on him. The whiny one didn't want to be bothered with her, but to make amends with the fat one, she washed his clothes and shoes out in a creek. Later, he complained that the shoe leather shrunk up and made his bunions sting.

They bound her with rope at night and around her waist by day so she could keep walking to Cincinnati to get the train. She didn't care nothing about no bunions since she had foot problems of her own. She'd thought she'd be walking north, not north and then back south. The soles of her feet were like shoe leather, and she hoped they stayed that way. The warm weather meant the skin on her feet wouldn't crack.

They made slow progress on the train to Washington D.C. She was goods, so they tied her up in the goods car, and watched her like a hawk. They had sold her friend for travel money, so instead she let the handsome face of Lawyer enter her mind.

What a fine-looking man he was. That was part of her problem. She'd told him she didn't have no room or time to be cozying up to someone like him.

The middle core of her warmed in humid July to remember how it was to lie next to him in the Cole barn. That's what a free life would be like. Well, not lying in a barn, but lying next to the one you love, keeping each other warm.

She shook her head to clear it.

No way one such as him could love her. He was too fancy and she too plain. Tears smarted in her eyes when she thought of him going back to Ohio, seeing her gone, and knowing he was in debt to that Henry man she didn't trust.

The tears came down her face, because now he was a slave to a white man too. No different.

All because of her.

If she ever saw him again, she would be sure to tell him how sorry she was. But she knew she wouldn't see him. He had to be back on his way to Ohio now, so he could take his big test.

Take care of him, God. Hope he does well.

It was all she could do for him.

The closer they got to Milford, the more the slave catchers left her alone. When the train reached Crumpton, they saw fit to clean her up. They bought her a new skirt and shirt and told her to wash up in the creek bed. She knew why they cared. If she looked bad, beat up, or hurt, Mr. Milford might take it out of their prize money. They didn't want none of that. They wanted every penny.

Time to make herself look good, but it wasn't for the Milfords. She wanted to look nice for her mam and her brothers and sisters. They had to know she was okay, even if she wasn't around Lawyer anymore. She would inform them of her adventures up north so maybe some of them or their own would leave Mr. Milford poor and broke.

Realie would look good before she had to pay the price for running away. Her fingers turned cold, thinking about being put in the sweatbox in July. Would she make it out?

Her feet were mighty glad when they reached the large front yard of the Milford place the next afternoon. Milly came running out, with Calla right behind her, and started to scold her. Her talk was like a little hummingbird flying about her head. Realie plastered a fixed smile on her face and nodded.

"Some adventure you had, Aurelia?" Mr. Milford's face was all long and sad looking. As if he cared about her adventures.

She was supposed to lower her head and match his tones, but just as she was about to, she looked up instead of down.

All of her dear family was gathered in the front yard, but one person pushed his way through. Lawyer. He stood next to her Mam with a baby in her arms. He cut a fine figure in his breeches with a slave's loose work shirt on.

He opened his arms to her. "Realie. How I've missed you."

She tried to run to him, but the rope held her back.

Lawyer stepped forward and pulled at the other end, yanking the fat slave catcher to the ground.

Her family started hooting and laughing at him, but Lawyer wasn't laughing. He freed her from the rope and scooped her up in his arms, a nice safe place where she was meant be.

The fat slave catcher got up, sputtering. "Did you see how he did that? What you going to do?"

He quieted when Mr. Milford counted through a large wad of bills, ready to pay them both.

"I'm happy to see you, Realie. How's your arm?"

"Healed up, Lawyer, thank you. I'm sorry I ran off. I'm not running anymore. I've learned my lesson."

"I have, too. I'm getting you back to Ohio. We need to leave as soon as possible."

"To make your test?" Even though she knew it wasn't possible. Tears pulled at the corners of her eyes at all his hard work getting messed up.

He clasped her hands. "None of that matters. I bought your freedom. You're a free woman, Aurelia."

She pushed back from him. Out of habit, her eyes went to Milly Milford who focused her narrow blue gaze on her. Her eyes slid to Mr. Milford. Maybe he had something to say.

He nodded, not looking as mad as his wife, his face almost kind. "It's true. You belong to Mr. Charles Henry of Ohio."

"Which means," Lawyer said, his voice low, "you belong to yourself. And can do as you please."

She stepped from his hold and looked all around at her family. Her mam stood there with her new baby girl. Mam held out the baby with tears streaming down her cheeks. "Here's your sister. Name's Sally."

Realie took the baby and rocked her for a minute before giving her back, not wanting to get too close. Wouldn't do when she didn't know what was going to happen to her. Looking into the round face of the baby gave her hope and she didn't need that right now. It was the same reason her mother didn't want to hold her either. She understood.

"What you going to do now, Realie?" Mam clutched at little Sally until she squealed.

"She's got to get out of here. Owner lives up north," Milly said, mean-like. "We've moved on without her."

Her blue gaze covered them all. Then she turned on her heel and went back into the house. She stepped toward her sister, Calla, but Calla gave a little wave and followed Mrs. Milford. She had to. That was how she would survive.

She had to leave. For her own survival.

"Okay if I leave with you, Lawyer?"

He gave her a shy smile. "Certainly. I'm hoping you'll come back to Ohio with me. As my bride."

Her hands got all sweaty all of a sudden. "You meaning me?"

He gripped her sweaty hand and didn't seem to mind. "I'm meaning you."

Her mother handed off the baby to Noah and stepped forward to embrace her. Finally. "Praise Jesus!"

Realie let go of her mother's soft flesh and turned to Lawyer, grasping his hands as firmly as the sweat on her hands would let her. "I sure will. I may not cook well, but I can help you so you pass your exam. So you can take it next time."

"I'll surely pass with such wonderful support."

One of her brothers, probably Sam since he was the noisiest, yelped, and everyone surrounded them and gave their congratulations.

Mr. Milford stood there, watching them. What did he want? Why didn't he go back into his nice cool house with his wife?

He stepped into the circle of her family, and they all quieted. "If you want, Realie, I'll be happy to perform the ceremony. Here, with your family."

She turned to Lawyer, really Lawrence, who was to be her husband. "What should I do?"

"Whatever you want. I know you'd want to have your family see you married. We can do it here and in Ohio."

Since she, as a slave, couldn't marry in Georgia.

It was tradition that Mr. Milford married their slaves under the marriage tree on his front lawn. God's holy church.

She was fine with it.

Mr. Milford held up a hand. "I call an afternoon of celebration in Realie's honor. I'll see what the cook can rustle up."

Mr. Milford went inside to tell his wife. In a minute, she and Calla rushed back outside.

"I love a slave wedding. Oh, thank you, dear," Milly called out to her husband, clapping her hands. "You knew what to do. It was so boring around here."

Realie stepped up to hold out a hand to her younger sister, squeezing it. Calla's hands were soft now, but they would roughen in time. Calla was going to have to do every little thing Milly wanted from this point on. Poor thing.

In an hour's time, her sister had created a beautiful floral wreath for Realie to wear. Her father led her to a spot beneath the spreading branches of the marriage tree, the swaying branches cooling them just a bit in the fierce Georgia heat. There Mr. Milford opened his Bible and read words, marrying them to her mother and father's satisfaction.

No more nights in a slave cabin, no more. She had promised herself that much when she left, and Lawyer—bless him—helped her keep that promise.

Riding in the wagon to the dock, Realie told her new husband how sorry she was that he'd missed his big test. Lawrence only smiled. "I've learned so much in the past weeks about what freedom and liberty really mean. Meeting you has given me a purpose I never had before. So don't you apologize. It was my luckiest day when I met you. I'll be a real lawyer, one day. Right now, I'm your Lawyer. That's enough for me."

"I'm a better woman too." She hunched up her shoulders, bubbling with laughter inside. "I never thought I'd get married."

"God takes us on all kinds of journeys, Realie."

"This'll be the last one I'm taking. Thanks be to God."

He scooped her up in his arms and placed a kiss on her lips, as delicate as the jouncing wagon would allow. With his smooth, sweet kiss, she was truly free. He wasn't the lucky one. She was. Her liberated heart flew heavenward on bird's wings of joy.

AUTHOR'S NOTE

Slavery was a horrible, nasty business. Still, what I've disliked about the way the institution has been treated, as of late, is the tendency to dismiss its relevance in our history. Realie found freedom, but what must be realized is that she is still property. It's wonderful that she found love with her Lawyer, but in order to be with him, she had to be purchased. White abolitionist groups would often start funds to purchase the enslaved to freedom, when the law made it clear that African Americans would not be free in any other way. Even prominent formerly enslaved folks like Frederick Douglass and Harriet Jacobs had to be purchased to freedom. They both hated that white benefactors had to purchase them in order to make them free. However, let it be noted that Charles Henry did Lawrence no such favors. The struggling young lawyer took out a loan to purchase his future wife and every single cent must be paid back…..

Thank you for reading *The Lawyer's Luck!* I hope you enjoyed it. If you did, please help other readers find this book:

1. This book is lendable, so send it to a friend who you think might like it so she can discover me, too.

2. Help other people find this book by writing a review.

3. Sign up for my new releases e-mail by contacting me at *http://piperhuguley.com.* Fill in the "Contact Me" information so you can find out about the next book as soon as it's available. There you may also find blog about the history behind my stories. Feel free to share links and/or tweet about posts that interest you.

4. Come like my Facebook page. Piper Huguley.

5. Join the Milford College Facebook group to keep informed about the building of a tradition over time.

Coming in July 31, 2014
The story of Realie and Lawrence's daughter

1866 – Oberlin, Ohio

Devastated by her father's death days after her triumphant graduation from Oberlin College, Amanda Stewart is all alone in the world. Her father's unscrupulous business partner offers her an indecent proposal to earn a living. Instead, to fulfill a promise she made to her father, she resolves to start a school to educate and uplift their race. Sorting through her father's papers, she discovers he had carried on a mysterious correspondence with a plantation in Milford, Georgia. She determines to start her teaching work with the formerly enslaved. However, when she arrives, the mayor tells her to leave. There's no where for her to go.

Virgil Smithson, Milford's mayor, blacksmith and sometimes preacher man with a gift for fiery oratory, doesn't want anything to do with a snobby schoolteacher from up North. On top of everything else, the schoolteacher lady has a will hard enough to match the iron he forges. He must organize his fellow formerly enslaved citizens into a new town and raise his young daughter alone. Still, his troubled past haunts him. He cannot forget the promise he made to his daughter's mother as she died—that their child would learn to read and write. If only he didn't have secrets that the new schoolteacher seems determined to uncover.

To keep THE PREACHER'S PROMISE, Amanda and Virgil must put aside their enmity, unite for the sake of a newly-created community in a troubling age, and do things they never imagined. In the aftermath of the flood that was the Civil War, God set his bow upon the earth to show love and understanding for humankind. To reflect God's promise, these combatants must put aside their differences and come together--somehow.

Oberlin, Ohio- 1866

Amanda Stewart had nothing but the clothes on her back.

Ladies were not allowed to take Tabulation courses at Oberlin College, but she understood the red underlines at the end of the column of figures.

She needed to ask anyway.

"There's nothing?" Her Leghorn bonnet made it a little more difficult to lift her head, but she had to get a clearer view of her father's law partner, Mr. Henry.

And instantly regretted looking to him. Slimy Charles Henry made his way around to her side of his desk, to provide an intimate explanation to her, a newly impoverished daughter of Ham, just what it all meant for her.

The weakness in her stomach brought across her new reality plainly enough, and she clenched the folds of her crisp bombazine black mourning dress into her wet palms. At least gripping the material would dry her sweaty palms and give her wrists some strength. She needed strength now. *Help me through this, God.*

Reduced now to this new status—that of a poor russet-brown colored woman with a brand new college degree,--she adjusted the new bonnet but the gesture provided no comfort. She would have to endure the moist explanations of Mr. Henry straight into her delicately coiled ear, just above the tourmaline earbobs that her father had given her last birthday.

"Miss Stewart, your father was an abolitionist who saw to it that every penny that he had went to ending slavery. And he succeeded. That evil has been removed from the face of the earth in keeping with God's holy principle of thou shalt earn thy own bread from thine own sweat."

He sat up from his explanations and she bit the inside of her cheek to keep from laughing. Mr. Henry pulled out a handkerchief that had seen better days and mopped down his pink brow with it. The yellowing handkerchief made a trip around Mr. Henry's rather round and bulbous head soaking up all of the excess moisture on his face, head, and neck. By the time the cloth emerged, it was brown. Her desire to laugh decreased immediately.

"Yes, Father's cause has won the day. But he always saw to me and made sure that I was comfortable."

"Aloysius Stewart loved you much, child. He made sure you had the finest clothes, books, lessons to play the piano, deportment, and the, well, craziest idea of you taking the college course at Oberlin. Well, my goodness, that was certainly a waste of his money wasn't it?"

His recounting of how much her father loved her, combined with his recent passing a few weeks ago and now this horrible situation of her impoverishment caused her to bring out her own embroidered handkerchief.

His insult only hit her after she had wiped at the small tears at the corners of her eyes.

"Mr. Henry, my father was not just a fighter for slavery but an ardent believer in the strong hearts, minds, and bodies of women.

He saw to it that my mother had her own education before he married her. When my mother died, he vowed he would do the same thing for me." Amanda pocketed the handkerchief again since the desire to cry went away as she addressed his slight to her intelligence.

"Oh my," Mr. Henry slid himself around and sat on the corner of his desk, facing her. His posture was most inappropriate, but propriety for her feelings didn't matter, now that she was defenseless and poor. His shift in bringing his oily person closer to hers made her heart pound hard beneath the high collar of her bombazine. "I surely did not mean to offend, Miss Amanda, I did not. I just wanted to you to know. Of my concern for your present situation."

She fixed him with a gaze. "I appreciate your concern, but I only wanted what rightfully belonged to my father out of this practice. My Oberlin education has not afforded me the luxury of being a lawyer."

His blue eyes blinked in surprise at her. "Oh, ho. Miss Amanda. A lawyer? What??" And he backed off from her, wiping his eyes and bending over double in laughter at the preposterous thought.

She sat in the chair stiff, watching her father's law partner amuse himself at her expense, all of the while calculating, turning over in her mind what she had, and what she could keep. She had some other dresses would could be sold and that might be enough to live on for a while. It was a mere turn of a phrase for her to be a lawyer, of course, but what could she do with her new Oberlin degree? She didn't want to nurse. The smell of blood made her faint. And nurses had to deal with unwashed bodies. It was enough to deal with Mr. Henry's less than fastidious grooming at this point.

Mr. Henry straightened up and wiped at his eyes with his soggy brown handkerchief. "Yes, well. What to do, what to do? Aloysius had no other family and neither did your poor mamma. Are there any young men on the horizon? Marriage, perhaps?"

"Marriage?" She nearly hooted out the heinous word, but that was not proper behavior.

Her stomach would have turned over and plunged to her shoes if her stomach weren't already there at the limited prospects of her new life

"Yes, some one over to the college you've been attending class with. I mean, while you attended the Ladies course."

"I attended a Gentleman's course or two."

"You did? Oh my. Well, no matter that. Any possible candidates?"

"No." Even if there were, she wasn't sure she should tell him.

Mr. Henry arranged himself behind his desk. "Well, that's too bad. A properly educated dusky maiden such as yourself should be taken proper care of. By someone."

The look in his eyes shifted in a way that Amanda did not care for. At all. His blue eyes narrowed and fixed themselves on the rounded shape of her bombazine basque.

Every drop of blood in her body plummeted to her toes and she stood up, so that the blood would somehow shoot back up to the rest of her body against gravity. She must cease this regard her father's law partner had for her person. "I am not interested in marriage. And since I'm a Christian woman, the only arrangement I could be interested in would be marriage. I may have a brown skin tone, Mr. Henry, but I will be no man's soiled dove."

The smirk on his features quickly departed. "Yes. Well. Marriage would be the only thing for you."

"I couldn't marry for anything other than love, Mr. Henry."

He spread his hands and she had never noticed before how well groomed Mr. Henry's hands were. For a man. Although her father had been a lawyer, his hands looked like that of a working man's until the day he died nearly two weeks ago. "An idealistic point of view in such a cold, cruel world. I pray you find the love you seek, but it will be difficult for one like you."

She moved her dress from beneath the desk and edged out to the door. "Good day to you, Mr. Henry."

"Good Day, Miss Amanda Stewart. Your father was a special man and he will be sorely missed. I wish you, the only offspring he had, the best of lives."

Before she knew it, she was on the other side of the door, outside in the spring air, knowing Charles Henry for a liar.

She had no evidence of his untruths. But the shaky feeling in the marrow of her bones set off all kinds of alarms within her that shot up and down her arms and legs, leaving her cold in the warm May air. He had not told her the full story.

She walked along front street of Oberlin back to the small house they lived to let and spent the next hour pawing through her father's papers for some evidence, some scrap of something to condemn Charles Henry with.

Nothing.

But the last envelope she grasped was a letter that came for him after his death.

Dear Aloysius Stewart,

We have heard much of your career in spreading the epistle of education among the Negro people. And in that cause, we would like to engage you to come to Milford, Georgia to the Milford plantation to teach the recently freed slaves reading and writing skills. Given the strength of your purpose, we have enclosed a train ticket for you to come. Please wire ahead to let us know of your arrival. Signed, Mayor Virgil Smithson.

Amanda clutched at the envelope. *Thank you, God.* She now had a purpose. The Missionary Society had come around to various classes at Oberlin all the time to solicit teachers of the race to go South to teach the newly freed brethren the skills in literacy. She had paid them no mind, because she did not need to. Then. And as for her father, didn't these people know that her father was a lawyer and not a teacher?

No matter, because as many times as she closed her mind to the opportunity before, this seemed to be the answer to her predicament now. The Missionary Society did not promise much money, but it was better than nothing and included a home to stay in and meals. She would sell off what she could of the books, but keep certain ones to send to the new school, as well as his diaries, which would be a comfort to her.

God's hand was in this. And in His mercy, He guided her gently away from the prospect of a horribly disgraced life to one encompassing pride and dignity. She rose on stiff knees and arched her aching back to send a wire to Mayor Smithson right away, lest he find someone else to take up the engagement.

Her father would be so proud of her—taking up the task of teaching the recently freed brethren how to read and write. Certainly a worthy work to take up in the name of God.

And, in the heat of Georgia, she would figure out some way to figure out just what Charles Henry was hiding from her.

"We late to pick up the teacher, Papa."

Virgil Smithson looked down into the bright black button eyes of his daughter and patted her on the shoulder. "I see, honey.

Had some extra customers to the shop. Couldn't be helped. The new teacher will wait on the platform."

March had put on her best dress, a white hand-me-down from one of the Milford grandchildren, which was too short. March tugged on it again, and her little spindly brown legs arched out from under the dress in a heartbreaking fashion. Where had seven years gone by so fast?

Her shoes were new at least, yet another reason why to take extra blacksmithing duties on. Won't have no one say his daughter didn't have wear shoes. She would be ready to go to the new school. He smoothed out the front of his black broadcloth suit, one of two he had befitting his new status as the mayor of a new town. His town. Milford, Georgia.

Carved out of the excesses of the large cotton plantation, Milford proper consisted of his smithy, a park in the town square planted with Mrs. Milford's favorite rose bushes, some resident cabins, and the train platform. Mrs. Milford was the only one who was left in the family in the main plantation house. The house, newly built after Sherman had come through, was not part of the town, but several miles due east. However, her imprint was there in the name and the rose bushes of the town.

Since Mrs. Milford believed in having Negroes lead their own, Virgil was her handpicked choice for mayor. His first act as mayor was to sent for and greet the town's first schoolmaster, come to Georgia to teach the free and the formerly enslaved to read and write. Mrs. Milford made that all possible.

And he hated every single second of it.

The school master would be the one to find out that he was the very last person in this hamlet of six hundred or so God-fearing souls who should be the mayor. Even as he approached the platform, his heart pounded at being found out.

But when he and March rounded the corner to where the once-a-day train dropped off cargo and people and chugged on to Savannah, there was no schoolmaster waiting on the platform.

Instead, on the train bench, sat the most beautiful lady he had ever seen.

He would have been no less surprised if a colorful parrot or macaw from one of the Milford grand children's picture books came and lit on the wooden bench.

March took in a deep breath and he put his hand on her shoulder to steady her. His little daughter trembled at the sight of the lady.

His own stomach pitched around like ash at the edge of the fire. The lady leaned forward to regard them both. Her skin was the medium brown color of cooked oatmeal, the kind someone else made and not him, since he tended to scorch it.

And she flashed a smile to them with small, even teeth of the pearliest white.

Her cheeks had dimples that sunk in so charmingly he would have sworn his heart flipped upside down inside of his chest.

But almost as spectacular as she was in face, she was surrounded by yards and yards of black dress material, a dress so big and wide with hoopskirting, she tamed it down with small dainty hands as she stood to greet him.

Her black bonnet bobbed in kind as she greeted them with a pleasantly voiced "Good Day to you."

"She's so pretty." March breathed in.

She must be the schoolmaster's wife. Such a beautiful lady must be married to a high-up man like a school master. Where was the schoolmaster? No one emerged and instantly, he was made a fool in front of this beauty. He would have to speak to confirm it.

"Ma'am. We're here to meet the schoolmaster. Is he 'round this way?"

She regarded him with large eyes that resembled the candy chocolate drops Mrs. Milford kept in a big jar in the parlor. Her eyes were merry. "Are you Virgil Smithson?"

"I am."

He did not put out his hand as it would not be appropriate to shake hands with another man's wife. He had a daughter to raise and did not want to start trouble with the schoolmaster first off.

"I'm Amanda Stewart."

Virgil nodded. A nice proper name. "And your husband is getting your trunks?" Although it made no sense, a trunk should have been unloaded with them, but he saw nothing.

"I have no husband, sir. And I have no trunk."

"Your black dress?"

"For my father. Aloysius Stewart. I'm his daughter, Amanda. I've come to be the schoolteacher."

A rush of blood came into Virgil's ears and his heart threatened to beat right out of his chest.

"You? A schoolteacher?"

The lady, she said her name was Amanda? She rearranged her big skirt, big like how Mrs. Milford's used to be, and put her gaze on him. Something about her eyes, made her look as hopeful a little girl as March. "Yes, thank you Mr. Smithson. I've just finished the course at Oberlin College in Ohio. I've been my father's pupil for many years before that. Let me assure you, I'm well qualified."

"We wanted a man. Where is he?" Virgil blurted out and red heat blossomed onto his neck and face. She was sure to see it, no matter the deep brown of his skin tone. "Oh. So sorry for your loss."

The look on her delicate features etched deep pain. If she had been punched in her the gut, she would have looked as hurt.

He wanted to collect her up and tell her it would be all right. "I'm sorry for your loss, miss." And he was sorry, but there was some terrible mistake.

"Thank you." She pulled a delicate white hanky out of a skirt pocket within the big skirt and wiped at her nose with it.

The whiteness of her hanky contrasted sharply with the deep jet of her gown and Virgil almost forgot his daughter in his discomfort until March said, "Pretty lady teacher."

And before he could stop it, Amanda Stewart bent down to talk with March, her big wide skirt spreading out into the dusty wooden platform. "Hello, I'm Miss Stewart."

"Pleased to meet you, Miss Stewart."

She bestowed that smile of hers on his little daughter and a connection knit itself between the lady and his child. No. Time to cut this off. He took March's hand in his. "The community sent for a male teacher, Miss."

Amanda stood and faced him again. This time he was surprised that the tip of her bonnet just about measured up to his chin. She carried herself much bigger than that. Or maybe it was her clothing. "You are mistaken, sir. The missive said you needed a teacher. I can provide that service."

He let go of March's hand and pointed down the road. "Most of them who needs the lessons is going to be old and big. Case you hadn't heard, freed slaves want to read and write. Got to stand up to them and not have no tinies talking to them just so."

He was a man who saved his eloquence in defense of God, especially when he prayed. He didn't know how to talk to some fancy Northern schoolteacher lady.

"Mr. Smithson. What are *tinies?*"

"Well, now..." Virgil spread his hands.

"Someone like me, ma'am. Small. Getting in the way. Daddy calls me a tiny sometimes. But I'm March. Mamma name me that so I know when I was born."

The lady inclined her head and looked down at March, her bonnet bobbing. "No tiny you, my child. You are a big girl. Even I can see that. A lovely spring child, just like your mamma named you."

"Got lots to do," Virgil interrupted. Wasn't too good for March to get big notions in her head. "And I don't have no time to watch over no schoolteacher lady."

"There have been women schoolteachers all over the South before and after the war, Mr. Smithson. I have my letter from the mission right here."

Virgil held up a hand. "I don't need to see no letter. And those women are widows. Or married. White ladies."

March coughed into the stillness.

And it lay between them.

The cast of her skin lit from within, shone incandescent. The recent loss in her life showed in the deep wells that showed sharp cheekbones above the dimples. Did she have Indian blood? A mixed-blood lady teacher would have an even harder time. No, she had almost got him, but she had to go home. He picked up her case. "Well, I get you on to Pauline's and get you comfortable for the night. Bring you back here to meet the train in the morning."

If he had shot March with an arrow, he couldn't have wounded his daughter more, judging from the screwed-up look on her brown face. And made him all the more determined for this pretty lady to get on about her business. This woman with her fancy bonnet and her big trailing dress with the smallest possible waist put big ideas into March's head. What would he do with that once this lady was gone on about her rich life? Best to put all of that to an end. Now. Today. Well, at least tomorrow.

He moved off the platform, and March dragged her feet in her dusty shoes. But the rustle of the lady's skirts did not follow them.

Virgil turned. She was still up there on the platform, a dark bell against the afternoon sky.

"Got to walk. Town's up this way, Miss. Can't wait out here all night." If she stayed all night on the platform, he really would be responsible for her then. The thought of what could happen to her in the night made his dry throat catch.

"I'm staying right here, Mr. Smithson."

A stubborn female. An even worse sight for March to see.

He started again. "Nightfall come, Miss, and the night riders could come and do you great harm. Wouldn't want it to come to that."

Couldn't she see her safety was at stake? And he couldn't touch her to bring her on. He looked at March to see if she was concerned about this lady's safety, but his daughter, his own child, looked away from him.

Miss Amanda embodied danger itself. She had to go.

"I mean to say, I can't go anywhere else, Mr. Smithson."

"I'm telling you, Pauline will put you up. What else you need to know?"

"I'm homeless, sir. I have no home or family or anywhere else to go."

He dropped her case to the dust, clean out of options and responses. No matter that he was a freeman who bought himself out of slavery way before the war come. A man who used fire to make iron bend to his will had just met his match.

"We going to find the right place for you to stay, ma'am," March told Amanda.

"Hush up, gal," March's father said.

What was his name again? Virago... no, Virgil. Virgil Smithson. She could not reconcile the tall, fearsome bearded man in the pressed broadcloth suit with the name signed on the paper.

In person, he appeared like the picture of God on judgment day that used to be in the back of her primer. That book scared her silly for a good bit of her childhood, and it was probably a reason why she was not proficient to this day in that particular subject.

March squeezed her hand tighter, and the child's bones pressed with a sharpness. Had the child had a decent meal? Her heart plunged into her throat at the way the child had tried to dress herself up to meet her. March was not well-put together. Did her father have something to do with the awkward tilt of her braids and the shortness of her patched-together dress? Where was her mother?

Her thoughts could not linger long on those suppositions, because the hem of her black gown grew increasingly red with dirt as she walked. She hiked her skirts up a tad, but Virgil Smithson stared at her with a stern frown that made his mustache and small beard glint in the sunlight.

"Ladies wearing dresses like that don't walk in the dirt 'round here. They ride. Not a good use of dress."

"Well, sir, I wore what I have. I must wear mourning for my father."

He grunted. Grunted? Not very pleasant behavior, that. For a mayor. She tried to rearrange her face in a posture that did not judge, but she could not help herself. Father had been so refined a gentleman that she was not used to men who grunted, but she supposed they existed in this world.

He stopped walking, and they stood there in the middle of a roughly-hewn town square. The pink flowers along the edges certainly pleased the eye.

"What we doing, Papa?"

"Supposed to take the schoolmaster up to Mrs. Milford. She ain't him, so there's no need."

"I admit to a bit of train grime and some of this Georgia dust, but I assure you I will not embarrass anyone."

"She's a beautiful lady, Papa!" March fairly shouted.

"Thank you, honey." Amanda looked down into the sweet brown face of her new friend. It was good to have someone who cared, even if she was only six or seven years old.

"Won't take her on up to the Milfords looking like that."

"And how do you suggest I look, Mr. Smithson?"

He stared about him, paying her no attention. If the day weren't already so hot, she believed her blood would be near-boiled at his near-direct accusation.

Silence.

She repeated her question, lest he have a hearing impediment of some kind.

"Pauline must be in the fields. We got to get her to help."

"I don't know who Pauline is, but I don't want her help. If there is a basin of hot water, that will be sufficient."

Virgil Smithson put her case down and began to whistle and wave his arms. At his command, a bunch of young men came forward and surrounded him, jostling for position. What kind of Negro man was he who commanded that kind of respect? He towered above the rest of them, certainly.

The young men surrounded him, and he spoke to them in low, hushed tones so she could not hear. On purpose.

Very disrespectful. She pressed her lips together. A good deal of alarm on his part had to do with her arrival and staying, and this impromptu gathering with young Negro men dressed in a variety of dirty overalls, shirts, and work pants was most irregular. One by one, they disbursed from him, but as they did so, they gave her sidelong glances as if she were some kind of china doll. Which she wasn't.

"I would like to freshen up please." She smoothed down her dress.

"Don't worry, Miss Lady," March informed her. "Papa just went to get Pauline to help you out of your present trouble."

She shook her head. "I'm not in any trouble. I just want to get to the house set aside for the teacher, so I can refresh myself. I have not come to be any trouble. I want to help." She squeezed the thin, small hand. "And my name is Miss Stewart."

"Miss Stewart. Hello." March tilted her head as she appraised her once more and threw her thin arms around a side portion of her skirt.

Amanda pulled the child's shoulders closer to her. Her heart did flips. She could feel March's shoulder blades through the white cotton dress she wore. "I believe it is time for some sustenance of some kind."

Virgil Smithson just stood in front of them, arms folded. He pulled out a pocket watch and frowned. "Pauline be here soon."

If this man were the mayor, didn't he do anything himself? And who was this Pauline? His wife? Would he call his wife by her Christian name in front of her?

At the very thought of it, she breathed out a little, pressing on a stay stabbing her in the ribs and near determined to break through her corset. Virgil Smithson was a handsome man for women who liked that fierce, thundercloud kind of look. His eyebrows looked like raven's wings over his dark black eyes and surprisingly long, lush eyelashes. His cheekbones sunk in deep, and his beard and moustache were trimmed neatly. Everything thing about him, his derby hat, and his Prince Albert broadcloth suit proved him to be well-groomed and reflected on him as a personage in charge. An authority. His height helped too. His carriage resembled a tree—firm and direct. Probably just as reassuring to... to Pauline. Whoever she was. Amanda surely did not care.

They heard a small scuffling and flurry, and from around the corner, a little woman in a simple blue dress and spotless white kerchief came forth. She wore a beautiful bandana on her head and carried herself as a regal person would. Almost as regal as Virgil Smithson.

The woman went right up to Amanda and grabbed her hands. It was impossible to tell how old she was, but surely, in her height, she was only a few inches taller than March and came up to Amanda's elbow.

"You the schoolteacher?"

"I am. Are you Pauline?"

"Yes, child. Wonderful to have you here. Come on to my home and we'll freshen you up some. Can't have you looking just anyway, not when you so pretty, just come from the cold North and all."

Her insides warmed at Pauline's words. It was good to be welcomed and not treated as if she had a dread disease. "Thank you." And Pauline let her hands go to stand on the other side of her.

"She need to change out of that dress and put on something right." Virgil followed. "Then she can get on that train and go back where she come from."

"Virgil. This here is women's business. I don't see where you need to put your oar in the water to start rowing."

"Yes, ma'am." Amazed at the respectful tone in Virgil's voice, this woman seemed to be more of a mother figure. If Pauline was not his wife, who was?

"Get on back to work," Pauline directed him. "We'll see you at suppertime up to my house."

Scurrying off between a small child and a small woman, her limbs lifted light in the air, so she stuffed her hands full of her dress to keep them stationary. *Thank you, God. I've been taken over so quickly in this strange place.* Still, she could not resist a look over her shoulder at the left-behind figure of Virgil Smithson who stood like a terrifying tree with his pocket watch in his hand, eyebrows drawn together as if judgment day was just around the corner.

There was a lot he had to learn about someone like her if they were to get along. Then again, she didn't come down south just to teach the children—she came to teach anyone who wanted to be taught.

Virgil could be first on the list.

Virgil had only returned to Milford last year, too long no doubt, but people here acted fool crazy over this so-called schoolteacher with the big skirt.

Come stepping off of the train, thinking she's Mrs. Abe Lincoln or somebody high up. In all his born days, he never had seen anyone like this woman. She made his head hurt and a strange, quivery feeling start up in his stomach like he ain't had nothing to eat in days. Which wasn't true, because ever since he had come back, Pauline saw to it that he and March ate very well, which he paid her to do. Still, March was too thin and small for a child of her years. He meant to have her be fattened up.

Had Mrs. Milford cared for March while he was gone? To take over his daughter?

No time to think on that now. He ought to do as Pauline say and get back to the shop. If there wasn't a couple of horses to be shod, he probably had mayor business to see about.

And he would do it too, if it wasn't for this lady come in on the train playing fancy in her mourning dress. How could someone who looked like that have to come down here to find a place to be in the world?

Her skirt disappeared around the corner to where Pauline had taken her, and his apprentice, Isaac, came up to him. "That the teacher?"

He pulled off his broadcloth coat and carefully hung it on the coat rack in the corner of the shop. It was a day to take off the shirtwaist to work, but he would just roll up the sleeves to the mid-portion of his arm. He didn't want to alarm anyone. His time away from Milford meant that he possessed a great deal of body strength, and he needed every bit of it to control the rages of his smithy.

The heat in the shop verged on unbearable, and he worked, drenched constantly in sweat, but at least the place was all his. It resembled the fiery pit of damnation, but he was proud of what he had accomplished. And he had accomplished it, despite great personal cost.

"Sent the wrong one. She need to get on the train back to where she come from and get on about her business up north." If he spoke it aloud, God would make it come to pass.

But she said she had no home. How could that be?

What had Miss Lady of the Bountiful Skirt accomplished? Anything in her spoiled, soft skinned, big saucer-eyed, soft-handed life? Probably nothing. A woman like that would melt down here in the hard South. And as mayor, this woman had become his problem. One that Mrs. Milford was not going to like or want to deal with.

"Line up these horses, boss?" Isaac said.

"Yeah. Ain't going to shod themselves."

"She was mighty pretty to watch, though. And got book learning. Why she have to go away?"

"Got to keep our minds on watching the fire and getting these horses taken care of. Can't be worried about no women just now."

"Need something pretty to look at 'round about these days."

Virgil fixed Isaac with a hard gaze, but his apprentice did not seem to mind. "Pretty is as pretty does. Nothing worse than a vain woman. And you got Pauline to look at. Mind that."

"I know. But she teaches folk to read. And, well, I never thought about learning to read. But if she's teaching the children, maybe..." Isaac's voice wandered off, still not paying proper attention.

"Maybe what?"

He didn't want the young man to cower. Virgil knew he had a stern way about him; it was one of the things Sally was always telling him about himself. But just now, Isaac was about too much good timing and not enough working. And here he had already wasted half the day, picking up this teacher who wasn't even what the community needed.

"Nothing, boss man."

"See to it. Bring in that filly. Horse needs proper shoes to make sure she working right. No extra time to be wondering about getting reading lessons. Do that on your own time."

"Yes, sir. Just thought, now we can do what we want, maybe we want to read."

"Read what? You learning a fine trade here. Been a free man blacksmithing all my life. Saved up enough money to buy my Sally up out of it. Ain't nowhere you can go where folks don't need a smithy."

"Smithing is a fine profession," Isaac echoed.

"Be sure you know it too."

"Man can't work all the time, though, sir." Isaac said it in the most pleasant voice he had. The lack of a smile on his face proved he meant what he said. "Man should make a nice living and then find a nice wife and get settled down somewhere. I wants to work for myself."

"Well, first you work for me," he told his apprentice, meaning to sound jovial. He failed miserably.

"Beg pardon, sir."

Isaac brought forward a dappled gray, petting her down her forelock, and handed the horse off. Virgil touched the horse's withers, reaching for a carrot to help calm her. He grasped her leg and put it in the target spot between his knees. A large part of smithing was getting the horses calm so their shoes could be changed without too much difficulty.

"God and a woman. That's who ought to boss a man," Isaac said with certainty.

Virgil nodded, determined to work.

"Milfords was okay to us and all, but we wasn't free."

"Wasn't around here enough to know." Virgil patted the horse down again. "Calm down, lady."

"Good thing. Sally slaved for that woman a long, long time."

Isaac's words stopped him. Anything stopped him when the talk was about March's mother.

"I know." He pulled the calm horse's hoof to him, and the gray let him hew the hardened nail away to pry off the old shoe. "I knows."

"Sally died not knowing what you done for her."

"She think..." He patted the horse to calm it. Well, and himself too. "She think I left her all by herself for good. That I was no good."

"Everyone know you be back."

"Georgia didn't let no free people stay. Couldn't stay with my wife and child, no matter how much I wanted." He wanted to pound a shoe so bad just now. But he was at the point of getting the horse's old shoe off. Without hurting this skittish lady.

"She knew. And that's how come Mrs. Milford ain't said nothing."

So Mrs. Milford's silence had met its goal—to divide him from Sally for the rest of his life. And if Mrs. Milford knew about this new lady schoolteacher, she would find a way to put a stop to that as well.

Which might actually work well for him. They'd be together on something for once. Pretty pampered thing like Amanda Stewart, she see how hard life was down here and she would forget all about teaching a school and go running back up to where she come from. He'd make sure of it.

He pried up the shoe from the horse's foot with an implement and pared away the hoof to get an even level. "Beat the shoe out."

He tossed the horse's shoe back to Isaac who caught it with the long pliers and laid it in the heat. His loud taps against the anvil rang out and echoed in the small old barn. Isaac stopped when the shoe was evened out and plunged it in the water to cool. Steam rose up from the water pit, and a twinge of discomfort plucked at him. Silence was a comfort usually, but the annoying thought about Amanda Stewart's presence stirred him inside.

"I don't want that teacher coming up in here ruining my daughter. Putting ideas into her head."

"How she going to ruin her? She can teach her things about being a fine colored woman, maybe teach her to be a schoolteacher."

Isaac retrieved the shoe and held it before him for inspection. Virgil shook his head, and Isaac laid it in the fire again, hammering hard to thin it out some more. He held it up again before plunging it into the water pit, and this time Virgil approved and took up the cooled shoe.

He had to put it to Isaac so he would understand. So that anyone would understand. "No. March stay here with her family." Blood family was too rare to find.

"You know Sally didn't want March doing all her life for Mrs. Milford. She want her to learn to read and write. You promised her before you leave."

"Isaac. What you remember? You was just a tiny then."

"I'm March's uncle. Sally's baby brother. And I got to see that you do right by her child."

"I know." A tug of irritation pulled at him. Was it because Isaac sought to remind him that he was actually family to Sally and March and not just claim kin? Or was it because Isaac didn't do the shoe right the first time?

"God brung that teacher down here to help us. To help March. She'll bring something special to the place. You'll see."

If Mrs. Milford didn't first see that the younger woman was better dressed than her. And if she did... well, that would solve Virgil's problem, wouldn't it?

Somehow, the prospect didn't make him feel much better. The thought of the schoolteacher getting on the train to go out into nothingness, without a home or friend in the world, made his fingers stiff, not wanting to bend to work.

Retrieving the first shoe from the pit, and readying the nails to attach it, Virgil neglected to pat down the gray and she balked. Got to focus when working on a horse—they could sense turmoil going on in a man's mind, sure enough. 'Specially a female horse. He patted her forelock, and she calmed down.

Isaac had done a good job this time. Using five nails, he attached the shoe and when he let her leg down, he imagined the horse was grateful. He patted her to show he understood.

There had to be a way of helping Miss Stewart and being shed of her.

The horse's feet danced all around his, eager for relief to get her other shoes changed. He made sure to stay out of the way. Didn't need to be laid up with a broken toe or foot. Lots to do here, and a rumble of irritation stirred through his fingers. He was behind because of the time he took to meet the lady schoolteacher. One they didn't even need.

The gray kept on dancing and he patted her down. Better to focus on the grateful gray filly and the work ahead. He couldn't afford any more women coming into his life seeking to destroy him, including this here filly, impatient with her dancing sore feet.

He would figure it all out by supper time.